WHAT-THE-DICKENS

WHAT-THE-DICKENS

The Story of a Rogue Tooth Fairy

Gregory Maguire

CANDLEWICK PRESS

First paperback edition in this format 2009

The Library of Congress has cataloged the hardcover edition as follows:

Maguire, Gregory.
What-the-Dickens : the story of a rogue tooth fairy /
by Gregory Maguire.— 1st ed.
p.   cm.
Summary: As a terrible storm rages, ten-year-old Dinah and her brother
and sister listen to their cousin Gage's tale of a newly hatched, orphaned
skibberee, or tooth fairy, called What-the-Dickens, who hopes to find
a home among the skibberee tribe, if only he can stay out of trouble.
ISBN 978-0-7636-2961-8 (hardcover)
[1. Tooth fairy—Fiction. 2. Orphans—Fiction. 3. Storytelling—Fiction. 4.
Storms—Fiction. 5. Cousins—Fiction. 6. Fantasy.]   I. Title.
PZ7.M2762Wha 2007
[Fic]—dc22   2007024186

ISBN 978-0-7636-4147-4 (paperback)
ISBN 978-0-7636-4307-2 (reformatted paperback)

10 11 12 13 14 15 WCB 10 9 8 7 6 5 4 3 2

Printed in Depew, NY, U.S.A.

This book was typeset in Bembo.

Candlewick Press
99 Dover Street
Somerville, Massachusetts 02144

visit us at www.candlewick.com

It is equal to living in a tragic land
To live in a tragic time.
—Wallace Stevens, "Dry Loaf"

We live in the most brightly
illuminated of dark ages.
—Paul Heins, in conversation

– CONTENTS –

TWILIGHT

BY EVENING, WHEN THE WINDS ROSE yet again, the power began to stutter at half-strength, and the sirens to fail. From those streetlights whose bulbs hadn't been stoned, a tea-colored dusk settled in uncertain tides. It fell on the dirty militias of pack dogs, all bullying and foaming against one another, and on the palm fronds twitching in the storm gutter, and on the abandoned cars, and everything—everything—was flattened, equalized in the gloom of half-light. Like the subjects in a browning photograph in some antique photo album, only these times weren't antique. They were now.

The air seemed both oily and dry. If you rubbed your fingers together, a miser imagining a coin, your fingers stuck slightly.

A fug of smoke lay on the slopes above the deserted freeway. It might have reminded neighbors of campfire hours, but there were few neighbors around to notice. Most of them had gotten out while they still could.

Dinah could feel that everything was different, without knowing how or why. She wasn't old enough to add up this column of facts:

- ✦ power cuts
- ✦ the smell of wet earth: mudslide surgically opening the hills
- ✦ winds like Joshua's army battering the walls of Jericho
- ✦ massed clouds with poisonous yellow edges
- ✦ the evacuation of the downslope neighbors, and the silence

and come up with a grown-up summary, like one or more of the following:

- ✦ the collapse of local government and services
- ✦ the collapse of public confidence, too
- ✦ state of emergency
- ✦ end of the world
- ✦ business as usual, just a variety of usual not usually seen.

After all, Dinah was only ten.

Ten, and in some ways, a youngish ten, because her family lived remotely.

For one thing, they kept themselves apart— literally. The Ormsbys sequestered themselves in a scrappy bungalow perched at the uphill end of the canyon, where the unpaved county road petered out into ridge rubble and scrub pine.

The Ormsbys weren't rural castaways nor survivalists—nothing like that. They were trying the experiment of living by gospel standards, and they hoped to be surer of their faith tomorrow than they'd been yesterday.

A decent task and, around here, a lonely one. The Ormsby family made its home a citadel against the alluring nearby world of the Internet, the malls, the cable networks, and other such temptations.

The Ormsby parents called these attractions slick. They sighed and worried: dangerous. They feared cunning snares and delusions. Dinah Ormsby wished she could study such matters close-up and decide for herself.

Dinah and her big brother, Zeke, were homeschooled. This, they were frequently reminded, kept them safe, made them strong, and preserved their goodness. Since most of the time they felt safe, strong, and good, they assumed the strategy was working.

But all kids possess a nervy ability to dismay their parents, and the kids of the Ormsby family were no exception. Dinah saw life as a series of miracles with a fervor that even her devout parents considered unseemly.

"No, Santa Claus has no website staffed by

underground Nordic trolls. No, there is no flight school for the training of apprentice reindeer. No to Santa Claus, period," her mother always said. "Dinah, honey, don't let your imagination run away with you." Exasperatedly: "Govern yourself!"

"Think things through," said her dad, ever the peacemaker. "Big heart, big faith: great. But make sure you have a big mind, too. Use the brain God gave you."

Dinah took no offense, and she did try to think things through. From the Ormsby's bunker, high above the threat of contamination by modern life, she could still love the world. In a hundred ways, a new way every day. Even a crisis could prove thrilling as it unfolded:

✦ Where, for instance, had her secret downslope friends gone? Just imagining their adventures on the road — with their normal, middle-class families — made Dinah happy. Or curious, anyway.

✦ For another instance: Just now, around the corner of the house, here comes the newcomer, Gage. A distant cousin of Dinah's mom. A few days ago he had arrived on the bus for a rare visit and, presto. When the problems began to multiply and the result was a disaster, Gage had been right there, ready to help out as an emergency babysitter. Talk about timely—it was downright providential.

How could you deny it?

Therefore, Dinah concluded,

✦ A storm is as good a setting for a miracle
   as any.

Of course, it would have been a little more miraculous if Gage had proven to be handy in a disaster, but Dinah wasn't inclined to second-guess the hand of God. She would take any blessing that came along. Even if decent cousin Gage was a bit—she tried to face it, to use her good mind with honesty—ineffectual.

Hopeless at fixing anything. Clumsy with a screwdriver. Skittish with a used diaper. ("As a weather forecaster," Zeke mumbled to Dinah, "Gage is all wet: where is the clear sky, the sunlight he's been promising?")

Yes, Gage Tavenner was a tangle of recklessly minor talents. Who needed a mandolin player when the electric power wouldn't come on anymore?

But he was all they had, now. An adequate miracle so far.

"Zeke," Gage called, "get down from that shed roof! Are you insane? We want another medical crisis?"

"I was trying to see where the power line was down. . . ."

"And fry yourself in the process? Power is out

all over the county. Up there, if the winds get much stronger, you'll be flown to your next destination without the benefit of an airplane. Down. Now. And Dinah, get Rebecca Ruth off that picnic table before it blows over. I'm going to make another go at jump-starting the generator."

If Zeke had been the type, he would have cursed. Instead, he obeyed with a lot of stomping and slamming, while Dinah snatched up their baby sister. They all stood inside the sliding glass door of the breezeway. They watched their cousin make no headway whatever with the generator. Without a word they moved aside when he gave up and came back in.

Aimless and cross, they milled about in the kitchen. Dinah shook the Cheerios box for the tenth time, but there was nothing in it but shaken darkness. The spoiled milk had been flushed down the sink yesterday morning. The spoiled meat had been thrown out the back door last night. Today they'd wolfed down the last of the bread for lunch, with two teaspoons of peanut butter made to spread on six slices. There wasn't much left to eat but furniture polish. Still, trusting in providence, the Ormsby kids kept looking through the cabinets.

The storm resumed its own sound track—the droning wind swelled, and flotsam blew against the house. This for the third night running. Then a new sound. A whistle, or was it more of a wail?

"Preserve us," said Zeke, as if he feared the opposite.

"Banshees," said Dinah helpfully. She wasn't trying to be mean, nor in any way impious. She thought if she made it sound worse than it could possibly really be, this might comfort Zeke. (Daily her brother, more literally than their parents, expected an apocalypse of Biblical scale.) "Starving coyotes? No. Something better. Vampires blown off course."

"Said with such enthusiasm, Dinah," observed Gage. "It's probably only wind coming in at a new slant. Forcing itself through some chink in the chimney. The hens down at—what did you say her name was, Mrs. Golightly?—at Golightly's place are going to be relocated to Mexico, where they'll have to learn a new chicken language."

"Hungry vampires might be glad to intercept some flying chickens in the night. . . ." Dinah said. At this point, she supposed, she would almost be glad to do so herself.

Vampires? Zeke scowled at his sister, to say, Don't go all Goth on me. Superstitious, for one thing, and you'll only scare yourself worse.

"'Wild nights are my glory,'" said Gage. "Who said that?"

Dinah couldn't answer. And Zeke only knew scripture verses.

"Mrs. Whatsit." Gage answering his own quiz. *"A Wrinkle in Time."*

"Never read it," said Zeke in a definitive tone, meaning: And mostly likely won't.

"Let's hunker down in the living room," said Gage. "It'll be cozier there." The kids knew he meant to get them away from the reality of empty cupboards. They obeyed him.

Dinah was glad that they'd pushed the sofa against the front door as a protection against burglars. This left plenty of space in the middle of the room to play picnic or Israelites in the desert or the Donner dinner party.

"Come on, Rebecca Ruth," said Dinah, lugging her little sister into the front room. "Tomorrow's your big day. Tomorrow you're the birthday girl."

"Birfday cake," remarked Rebecca Ruth, who paid a steely attention to her own desires. "Birfday cake. Birfday cake." Rebecca Ruth was ready to be two. She didn't want to wait one more day for her cake.

"Rebecca Ruth," said Dinah brightly, "I made you a present out of modeling clay. A pretend cake. Do you like it?" She took her surprise off the mantelpiece and showed her sister.

Rebecca Ruth pursed her lips, unsure, but Dinah was still proud of her work. Since there was no real cake in the house (or sugar or eggs or flour with which to make one), Dinah had searched all morning and she had scrounged up one lone birthday candle at the back of a pantry drawer. She had stuck the candle in her statue of a cupcake.

She turned it in a circle so her sister could admire it all.

"Cake," said Rebecca Ruth, sounding unconvinced.

"You're not one year old anymore, not after tomorrow," sang Dinah with big-sister bossiness. "You're two. Let's practice. One plus one equals—"

"Cake," answered Rebecca Ruth, dismissing it. "Prezzies?" she said, more insistently. "Real prezzies." She meant with wrapping paper and ribbons.

"The cake is your present. A pretend cake!" But Dinah knew her present was a failure, and she couldn't maintain the false cheer. "Don't you like it?"

"You should've let me check out the store, Gage, when I suggested it," said Zeke. "I might've found us a packet of stale bagels or something."

"I wanted to go myself," said Gage, which was true enough. But the hour had never arrived that seemed safe enough to leave the children alone. Nor would Gage allow Zeke to make a solo foray to the stores on the commercial strip a half mile downhill from them, to see if the looters had left a cupcake behind. Not when the reservoir was cresting its rim.

Zeke said, "Sometimes no present is better than the wrong present."

"Now you tell me," said Dinah, tossing the fake cupcake into the fake fireplace.

As Rebecca Ruth began to sulk at the lack of decent birthday tribute, the gale wind smacked the house squarely. Through the picture window they watched the picnic table lift first one leg, then the other three, and fly off in the direction of a happier picnic ground.

"Rock-a-bye, sleepy-bye," said Gage Tavenner to the toddler, gathering her up. To Dinah's eye, Gage didn't have the right equipment to make a small kid comfortable; his chest was too stringy and his chin had gone scratchy with stubble. But Rebecca Ruth didn't complain. "Shall I get out my mandolin again and try a lullaby?" murmured Gage.

Politely, Dinah and Zeke avoided voicing an opinion.

"Dinah, you should've gotten some food from Brittney and Juliette when you went to say good-bye to them," groused Zeke.

"Their parents had already boarded up their house. If you had any friends, you could ask them."

"You know we're not supposed to go downslope without permission."

"I was being charitable, Zeke. Comforting the sick."

"I'll say sick," said Zeke. He snickered with a degree of superiority unusual for him.

"They were sick. Sick with worry!" insisted Dinah.

Gage just kept humming to Rebecca Ruth. He knew that sniping among children was a kind of unstoppable natural force, like winds and tidal waves. But, though Gage was a first-year English teacher, he was too recently a grown-up to tell the difference between the normal antagonisms of kids and this new misery of hunger and waiting in the dark.

Gage suspected that if Dinah considered him a miracle, Zeke would probably settle on the term "trial." Or "handicap." Gage could hardly blame him. Three days now. Three days going on four. How much longer would he be able to manage to keep their spirits up?

But then Zeke seemed a skittish sort. At the best of times he was a jagged-eyed kid. (Dinah thought her big brother often had the look of a battery-operated toy that had been left on all night: frayed, over-juiced, imprecise in its behaviors. Ritalin candidate, Dinah's secret friends had mused wonderingly, with perhaps a tinge of admiration. Dinah wasn't sure.)

Zeke defied Gage's suggestion that they all stay put by going to rummage noisily in the breezeway storage cupboard. The faithful had nothing to fear, he knew. But did that mean that the presence of fear in his heart was a sign of his failure at faith?

As the garden shed door banged a final time against its wall and tore from its hinges, Dinah sighed. Within reason, she was almost enjoying herself. Considering . . . well, considering what she could bring herself to consider—admittedly, she couldn't imagine things that were beyond her imagination.

Like where their parents were, by now.

"What a mess in the morning—practice for Armageddon," she said, using a phrase of her mother's to change the subject. "We'll be cleaning up all day long. That is, if the looters don't break in tonight and slit our throats while we sleep."

"Dinah." Gage's voice was suddenly testy. "I know my job as a language arts teacher hasn't prepared me to head up the local chapter of Emergency Management. But let's not talk about throat slitting in front of the baby, okay? She's at a tender age. For that matter, I'm still at a tender enough age, too, though it doesn't show."

"I'm only trying to make conversation," said Dinah, and there was some truth to this. What were they supposed to talk about? The weather?

Zeke arrived from the breezeway with a can opener in one hand and a surprised look on his face.

"Hey, what do you know? In the cleaning cupboard I found a small sack of groceries Dad must have forgotten to unpack. A while ago, maybe, but it's canned goods, and they never go bad. A can of cling peaches, and a jar of creamed carrots, and some tuna fish. We can open a restaurant."

"Western civilization is saved," said Gage. "Good going, Zeke."

"Tuna Peach Surprise with a side of creamed carrots?" said Dinah. "I believe in miracles, but that's stretching it."

"I'm only trying to help," said Zeke. "If you'd bothered to scrounge up some supplies when you were out gossiping with those bubblebrains you idolize—"

Dinah opened her mouth to protest—what really was so wrong about having downslope friends?—but just then the oldest tree on the property shrieked and split. It fell in slow motion, and the air instantly smelled greener and raw. The cloud of branches mashed up against the picture window. Ten thousand wet leaves faced them, as if pleading for entry. Luckily, Gage had duct-taped the window, so the broken glass only spiderwebbed; it didn't fall inward.

"That'll help," said Gage. "It'll provide a barrier against any stronger winds." He didn't sound as if he meant it, really.

Rebecca Ruth started to cry.

"'Wild Nights! Wild Nights! / Were I with thee / Wild Nights should be / Our luxury!'" Gage spread a blanket out before the fake fireplace, and he sat cross-legged on it, and held the toddler on his lap and rocked her while she bucked and resisted. "Ah, sweetie, you don't care for Emily Dickinson?"

Dinah said, "I think she's more upset at the thought of Tuna Peach Surprise for her birthday dinner."

Zeke turned and said, "It's not her birthday till tomorrow. Maybe we'll locate some more supplies by then. Maybe Gage'll let me go scavenging." He left to open the cans.

Rebecca Ruth wailed louder. The clouds hunched and thundered. Rain hit the corrugated roof like a spilling of metal spikes.

"This is a good storm," said Gage.

"I hate to disagree," said Dinah, "but I'm beginning to think this is not a good storm. This is a bad storm."

"Well, maybe we should light the candles now?"

"Candle," Dinah corrected him. "There's only one candle left. I mean, not counting the birthday candle. Is it dark enough?"

"By the time it gets darker, we'll be ready to sleep. We won't need it then." So Dinah took down from the mantelpiece the empty mayonnaise jar with the last emergency taper inside. The jar was partly lined with aluminum foil to double the flame's light.

"Have you ever seen anything that produced a mudslide like the one over near Cardiff Canyon Road?" she said. "You know what's there, don't you? The county cemetery. Can you imagine the coffins all popping up, their lids splintering from the pressure—"

"Dinah." Gage's voice was sharp.

"I can," she retorted, honestly and defiantly. "I can imagine it just fine."

"You're being wicked, Dinah," Zeke called from the kitchen. "Since Gage won't say it, I must. It's my duty. You'll call wrath upon this house if you don't watch your tongue. Govern yourself!"

"Stop talking like you-know-who, just because they're gone," said Dinah. "You think you're in charge. You're not. Gage is."

"Here, Dinah," said Gage, "you hold Rebecca Ruth. I'll do the match." With fiddly fingers, he tried to light the wick. His hands shook, so it took a few tries. Finally he put the jar on the floor so they could sit around it, campers at an inside fire.

Zeke came in with a tray. Lumps of food in unmatched dishes. No one was hungry enough yet to eat the plain, ugly fare, so Zeke set the tuna and baby food and cling peaches aside on a table for later, or never.

He sat down near Dinah: the candle gave a kind of permission.

They sat so close, and so still, that they might have been carved out of one block of shadow-flickered granite. Young Man and Three Children in Trouble.

"Have you ever known a worse time?" asked Zeke. The question was meant to be calm, but the way his chin ducked into the collar of his shirt was revealing. He shook as if he was cold, though the house wasn't at all chilly.

Gage took such a long time to answer that all three children looked up at him. Dinah thought that his face, in the flickering candlelight, looked even less adult than usual. This wasn't consoling.

"Don't lie to make us feel better," she said. "You can't remember a worse time than this, ever. Can you."

"I can," he protested. "I can remember. But it's a complicated memory. I'm trying to think of how to say it."

Rebecca Ruth had stopped crying and was beginning to chew on the nose of her favorite stuffed animal, a little white woolly lamb that she called Tiger. "Say," she murmured, though it was unclear whether she was speaking to Gage or to Tiger.

There was a sound like that of a demolition truck

in the valley below, only there could be no trucks on the interstate because the overpass had collapsed.

More tricks of thunder. Dinah gripped Gage's forearm.

"All right, I'll 'say,'" said Gage. "Gather round."

They already were gathered round, their expressions reminded him. Dinah ringed her knees with her arms. Rebecca Ruth had her thumb back in her mouth. Zeke, eager for diversion but wary by nature, said, "I hope this is a true story."

"I rarely trust myself to make statements about truth," said Gage, "but it's a real story anyway."

"Well, is it a story about you?"

Gage waited for a break in the wind before he answered. "Not at first."

WHAT-THE-DICKENS

❧ ONE ❧

To start with, he wasn't much to look at—literally.

I mean he was slight and small. I also mean he blended in. His arm webs were filmy, nearly transparent, and his skin was suggestible, like water. I suppose his circulation worked on a capillary system; his coloring could shift from pale to dark, and many shades in between. A limited talent for camouflage. Not enough to make himself invisible — nothing like that.

But he wasn't much to look at even when you could see him right in front of you, or when measured up against others of his kind. His head was flat in back and his nose was more beaky than perky. His hair flew everywhere, as if eager to get off his scalp. His neck was a toothpick, his arms toothpicks, his legs tooth-picks with big flattened feet. Most skibbereen have slender feet that come to a point, like sharpened pencils, like ballet folk on their ballet toes. But our hero's feet were made for walking.

I met him when I was ten. That's the story, really. But first I should tell you about where he came from.

He was hatched at the twilight of a day that had been marked by high winds. Yes, worse than tonight's — no kidding — the aftermath of a hurricane. But the gales, by now, were worn out. The humid air settled against the earth and didn't budge.

It's hard to say what he knew at first. Not many of us humans can report much about the day we were born unless we're told about it. But he wasn't human.

Bright? Well, bright enough. But he was—well—disadvantaged. The accident of his birth. He was a scrap apart.

He opened his eyes, would you believe it, alone, in an empty tin can that someone had tossed by the side of a stream. How he got there, he didn't know, and nor do I.

No, he wasn't dressed. Who would dress him? But skibbereen are born with filmy webbing that falls from their shoulders and waists. It clings to their slender forms, like a nightshirt made out of cobwebs. Provides the bare minimum for the sake of modesty.

He felt sick, but maybe he was only reacting to the smell lingering in the can—tuna fish packed in oil. Still, he wobbled to his knees and he tried to stand up.

He was small, even for a skibberee. Perhaps he was the runt of the litter he couldn't yet imagine.

He didn't speak. This was unusual: Most skibbereen can talk almost at birth. They infer a whole language system from the first welcoming phrases with which their loving mother greets them. But since our hero couldn't verbalize yet, his thoughts came in gleams of insight and clouds of emotion.

The can was standing on its side, like a wheel, and the lid had been opened with a can opener but was still attached by a small tab of tin. Enough light bled in around the hatch's jagged edges that he could see someone else in his world with him. It was only his reflection, but he didn't know that.

Instantly he felt less alone, and—isn't instinct a grand thing?—he grinned at the apparition, which grinned back at him in a good-natured way.

They both smiled back and forth. Back and forth.

Just as this was beginning to feel old, the skibberee's birthplace started to roll sideways and back again. Terrified and thrilled at the same time, the orphan pushed against the lid of the can, smacking in the nose a curious cat that had come waddling along.

The cat, a fierce and elegant creature though unlovely in her morals, had stepped out to inspect the world after the storm. She smelled an agreeably fishy smell, noticed the old tin can, and so she had stopped to investigate.

"Meow!" said the cat, outraged.

Meow? thought the skibberee, and tried out the language. "Meow! Meeee-ow!"

The cat backed up in astonishment, the better to regard what she understood to be a noisy scrap of tuna. She was surprised, and she believed she'd been made a fool of, which irritated her. But like most cats, she kept her opinions to herself. The skibberee had no idea she felt vexed.

He studied her as she settled on her capacious bottom to think things over. He admired how neatly she encircled her white fur boots with her white fur tail.

She seemed to pay him no attention. Instead, she set to licking her white fur coat. The evening light struck her polished identity tag.

The tag spelled out *McCavity*. Had the skibberee been introduced to spoken language by his mother, he'd have been able to read the word at once — for reading comes as naturally to these creatures as chatter does. But the letters only looked like scratches, and the cat's single comment of *meow* hadn't been enough to jump-start an entire language operation. As it was, McCavity lowered her chin against her collar, and the nametag disappeared into folds of fur. (Not to be rude, but this cat was a healthy eater.)

The skibberee had no words yet for *family* or *love* or *home*. His heart swelled, though, as the gorgeous white cat pinned him in her sights. He twisted his fingers, wishing there were someone who could introduce him to the cat.

I don't know what McCavity was thinking—if anything. But by long-standing family custom, she was a hunter.

The white creature gathered her strength. She growled low in the back of her throat. She swiveled her hindquarters as the muscles of her haunches tensed. The skibberee watched with interest.

Then McCavity pounced, startling the skibberee backward into the can. He felt graceless and stupid, but this stumble saved his tender life, at least for the time being.

McCavity leaped again, this time knocking the open lid back into place, trapping the skibberee inside. She hissed in fury. The skibberee heard the hiss but not the fury. He keened wordlessly, hummingly back to her.

This only seemed to stoke McCavity's appetites. She worked a claw into the seam made by the lid, trying to pry open the can.

The skibberee was heartened, thinking that his new friend was trying to rescue him.

But before the orphan could be released from his prison, McCavity's claw withdrew. The whole can lifted suddenly upwards. The skibberee fell against the floor of his home. The wind was knocked out of him, but he didn't lose his lunch, for he'd never had a bite to eat yet.

The lid flipped up on its hinge of metal. A glaring light dazzled the silvery inside of the can. "What the dickens—?" said a voice. "Ugggh. Is that a mouse? McCavity! You beast. Up to your old tricks."

The human hand shook the can, though on purpose or not, the orphan skibberee didn't know. He was tossed in the air. Neither widened human eyes nor narrowing cat eyes could track the arc of his flight, or see where he landed in a clump of skunkweed.

Mostly unhurt, he righted himself, to watch what happened next.

"You'll cut yourself on this lousy old tin can," said the human. "No more scavenging for *you,* pretty McCavity. That doesn't suit a pet of mine. Let's go home." Human hands scooped the cat up, and human hands imprisoned her. She couldn't wriggle free to pursue her affairs.

"Meow," said McCavity, and other words

that sounded like *meringue. Shebang. Harangue. Fissssssssssss.* As if she'd rather have a pet of her own than be one.

"You heard me. I know you have a thing for mice. You probably learned to sniff them out from your mother; you can't help it. Still, that's no reason to go scaring some poor baby mousekin lucky enough to survive yesterday's storm. Come on, you rascal. I'll give you a treat at home. A special present. You like presents."

The skibberee was winded and disoriented. But the human voice had done the thing that his mother's voice might have done, and that McCavity's voice couldn't: it had lit the fuse of language in him. And once lit, it began to burn.

"McCavity," he murmured (very, very softly, practicing; he didn't want to make a fool of himself). "McCavity. What a smart name. McCavity. Could be the name of a mother, though I don't seem to take after her much, being shy of fur and whiskers and the like. Maybe I'll grow them as I mature. Or maybe we're not related at all. That's okay. I can deal."

After a while he crawled to his hands and knees and called after her. "McCavity! I'm here! Don't go away!" But the cat's companion—the human—kept clomping away through the bracken at the side of a stream swollen with storm runoff.

"Wait for me!" called the skibberee.

They didn't hear, so they didn't stop.

He followed as best he could, trying to keep them in his sight, but can an ant keep pace with an antelope? The human and his pet disappeared, and the silence they left behind seemed mocking and total.

So the skibberee made his way back to where the can had fallen to the ground. He wanted to find his twin, and to use this new trick of language on him. Maybe he could teach his partner to talk, and they could discuss what to do next.

The basics. How to live. How to behave. And why.

And what might make a really good present for a cat. To win her over. To win her affection.

He examined the picture on the outside of the can, a grinning cartoon tuna leaping from blue waves. The fish sported teeth that appeared to be in excellent condition.

"Hello! I'm back!" called the skibberee. "And I've a name now: it's What-the-Dickens!

And with a name, a personality, I hope. I have a question for you about presents. Hello?"

His companion, alas, was gone. (Probably the can had fallen on the ground at an angle that no longer allowed for a reflection, but What-the-Dickens couldn't understand this.)

What-the-Dickens curled up on the floor of his humble lodgings and he tried to go to sleep. He was hungry without yet knowing that hunger could be slaked by food; he was lonely without yet knowing that loneliness could be slaked, too.

❧ ❧ ❧

"What's a skibberee?" asked Dinah.

"Ah," said Gage. "You'll have to wait and find out."

"A creature in a tin can," said Zeke matter-of-factly. "Very pretty, very silly."

"You don't like it, you don't have to listen," said Dinah. "But, Gage, tell me. What-the-Dickens? What kind of name is that?"

"Hyphenated," said Gage. "Like, um, Winnie-the-Pooh. Or Sam-I-Am."

"Sam-I-Am sounds like a big, loud hello," said Dinah. "What-the-Dickens sounds like a question."

"Yes," said Gage.

TWO

What-the-Dickens, perhaps, sounds like a question of a name — and why not? Maybe most names should be questions, at least at first, for how do we know if our names fit us until we live a little?

The lonely skibberee slept with his hinging capewings pulled around himself for warmth. He was cozy, but not cozy enough. He didn't know that most newborn skibbereen sleep in a heap with sixty or seventy or eighty friendly siblings, an arrangement that makes them all feel safe and warm.

He'd heard that McCavity accepted presents, too, so he dreamed of looking for a perfect present to give the cat. Before he could dream what the present might be, though, he woke with a start. Something was jabbing at him.

He rubbed his eyes and thought blearily, *It's McCavity's claw. She's come back to release me from my loneliness, even if I haven't thought up a good present yet.*

Then he woke up some more at the snap of a pair of bright yellow pincers that caught him by the leg.

It was the beak of a rust-throated grisset.

She gripped What-the-Dickens and dragged him forward through the opening hatch.

"Let go!" said What-the-Dickens. "I have other plans for this morning. I need to find McCavity. I want to apply to be her pet." The grisset paid no attention. Hauling the skibberee by one leg, she managed a lopsided ascent to her nest in a nearby bog maple.

When she got there, she dangled What-the-Dickens above her four nestlings.

The nestlings cheeped something that may have meant "Breakfast!" if it meant anything at all.

Yikes, I'm their *present,* he thought.

Now, you should know that the female rust-throated grisset is a small bird that doesn't blend in. She can't fly quickly or in a straight line. Her small claws are useless for anything other than perching. Her only defense is her lack of musicality. She is tone-deaf. (Eventually, a mama grisset's song stylings drive her nestlings out of the nest. This is how they learn to fly.)

For all her deficiencies, however, the female rust-throated grisset is a plucky sort. Sure, she dips when she should dive, she swoops when she might more profitably swerve. But she is loyal to her own. She feeds them breakfast.

The mama grisset lowered What-the-Dickens headfirst toward the oldest and hungriest among her baby grissets. Luckily, the baby grissets didn't like their breakfast present. They preferred raw worms.

Still, they were too young to be rude. They wiggled around in their nest and made room for him while the mama grisset supplied an aria. When it finally trailed off, What-the-Dickens politely murmured, "Bravo."

The mama grisset got as tender a look on her face as was possible given the predatory lunge of her beak and the gleam of her bulging, lidless eye. At once she forgot that What-the-Dickens wasn't born of her own egg, and so she flew off to find some other breakfast choices for her babies, including, now, him.

❧ THREE ❧

As soon as the mama grisset had disappeared, What-the-Dickens stood up and leaned over the side of the nest. "Look!" he said to his nestling friends. "A rescue committee of one!"

The baby grissets craned their scrawny little necks as far as they could. A patch of white fur slithered behind the green slats of fern.

The baby birds shrank back, trying to be invisible.

"Did you see that creature?" asked the skibberee. "She's looking for me, I bet. Isn't she a fine specimen of a friend, waddling along like that? McCavity! Up here!"

McCavity heard the voice. Perhaps she understood English and perhaps not. You can never be sure with cats. In any case, McCavity's nose had picked up the trace amounts of rancid tuna, for a fading stink still clung to the webbing of the skibberee. Now her ears confirmed the suspicion: she had found him.

The white cat put her paws onto the trunk of the tree and stretched. Her eyes, from this angle, were like oxidizing bronze: emerald sparks in warm, loyal gold.

I'd better face facts, thought What-the-Dickens. *I think I'm in love with a cat. Well, I'll just keep it to myself.*

He couldn't wait a moment longer. "Coming!" he shouted, and he tore a broad leaf off at the stem. Gripping its rim as a child grips a toboggan, he launched himself into the air.

It was a foolhardy gesture. So young, he knew nothing about aerodynamics, except how the heart could lift and lift.

Did he plummet to his death? No, he surfed the breeze. He was light enough not to drop like a stone. The leaf circled without overturning, and the skibberee peered over the sides.

He was startled by what he saw. Remember, he was only one day old himself, and he'd seen little of the world so far, and all of it from close-up. This was his first sense of the larger landscape.

How marvelously the world seemed to unfold, improbably, in all directions—forest this way, field that! A grey ribbon looping over the hills to the north (in time What-the-Dickens would learn it was a highway). Off in the distance to the west, a lowland bog choked with purple loosestrife. It was as complete a world as What-the-Dickens had hoped for. And a river ran through it.

But before he could glide into McCavity's waiting claws, he was plucked from his vessel by the mama grisset. She dumped him back in the nest with the other nestlings, scolding What-the-Dickens as if he were one of her own.

She sat on him to make him be quiet. He pounded his little fists against her feathery rear end, while McCavity began to make her way up the trunk of the tree.

No big surprise, then, that the mama grisset suffered an attack of nervous conniptions. Her melody lost track of itself and became a shriek. When McCavity was only six or eight feet away, the mama grisset began to thrash her wings, to screen her children and to blind the intruder. In the commotion, she knocked one of her own nestling babies out of the tree.

What-the-Dickens lunged to grab the baby grisset's tail. He was too late, and grabbed only air.

But the smallest grisset did something wonderful. First she tumbled, and then she opened up her little wings. Clumsily she coasted a few feet and came to rest on a limb in an adjacent tree, looking surprised at herself, and a little smug.

"I didn't know you *little* ones could fly, too," whispered What-the-Dickens. "Wow."

The white cat continued to climb, so the mama grisset took emergency measures. If her littlest nestling was ready, the rest would have to be ready, too. Without ado she launched the other three grisset siblings. One by one they wobbled to new perches, and, delighted with themselves, they all began to sing. (Given their family background, they stank at singing. But you can't learn everything you need to on the same day, not even if you're stuffed with talent.)

The mama grisset was as much a mama as she was a grisset, so she couldn't abandon What-the-Dickens to his fate, about which she had a better idea than he did. She took him in her beak one final time. This at least had the advantage of silencing her concerto.

"No!" cried What-the-Dickens. He struggled and began to weep. "No, no! My ride is almost here. My friend looks for me. How dare you? Unbeak me, and I'll bring *you* a present the next time. . . ."

The offer didn't help. The rust-throated grisset had made up her mind. She left by wing, dragging What-the-Dickens beneath her.

He closed his eyes against the wind, but he felt also as if he were closing them against the world, which now seemed to be full of emptiness. What good was the future if he didn't have a job as a pet to a minor deity in a white fur coat?

❧   ❧   ❧

By now the night had fallen, with a quality of blackness rarely seen in a suburban setting. It made the house feel crushed into itself, as if it were floating in space, separated from anything. Well, given the backed-up sewage lines, the dead phones, the collapse of the power grid, the Ormsbys *were* separated from everything.

Everything except themselves. While Gage went to refill his glass of water—to keep his busy voice from drying out—Dinah looked inquiringly at Zeke. *What-the-Dickens?* said her expression.

He rolled his eyes, indicating, *Stupid nonsense, but probably harmless.*

Dinah stuck her tongue out at her brother, signifying, *Don't be so superior.*

The usual conflict, and, in its way, consoling. They still had each other. That much was okay.

❧ FOUR ❧

The orphan skibberee was dizzy and lost. *What a mess I've made of my life so far,* he thought. *But where did I go wrong?*

He watched the feathery breast of his captor heave as the mama grisset flew on. He knew that she meant well. Sadly, her navigational skills were on a par with her singing talents. (Dismal.) True, she could manage to migrate south each autumn, and to make it back home again the following spring. But this was because she was usually accompanied by ten thousand other migrating grissets. When left to her own devices, she was hopeless. She repeated herself in circles.

Around and around the grisset swooped, over the cloverleaf, the scraps of woods, the abandoned millworks, the glittering string of river. Ten years ago, there weren't as many fast-food outfits in the outback of dairy country—remember, this is my childhood I'm describing. Sure, a few parking lots, the first of the strip malls converting patches of upstate farming community into suburbia—but not many. Instead, just weary old farms, outliving their usefulness. Village centers arranged a century earlier around the junction of railroad lines. Schools, of course, and playgrounds: there have always been schools and playgrounds.

But the biggest difference was the amount of undeveloped land. Hills weren't colonized: they were too hilly. Bluffs were left alone. No one wanted to build McMansions on the wetlands yet. There was more that was still wild back then, even in a settled district. We didn't crowd the world so much with ourselves.

The skibberee felt airsick. He thought they were flying a thousand miles. Every time they passed over the new county zoo, which had been erected not far from where one highway crossed another in a snarl of curving ramps, he thought it was another zoo. He could smell the warm stink of animal ordure, which he didn't mind, and hear the trumpeting of elephants, which he couldn't identify. "My, this world is huge, and full of noisy, windy creatures," he guessed. He was right about that, but for the wrong reasons.

The mama grisset didn't set out to abandon her passenger. She only wanted him to live long and prosper. She meant well when she decided to set him down on the lip of a jaunty old chimneystack three stories above the ground. She supposed that he could rest there and then fly away when he was ready. She thought the filmy webbing bunched up at his shoulder blades was a pair of wings.

But her aim was poor, and she dropped the poor skibberee right down the chimney.

I'm cooked, thought What-the-Dickens, tumbling into the dark. *I'm yesterday's news. How brief is life, how brief!* As he fell, he could hear the beginning of the mama grisset's song, now that her beak was available for use again. It sounded, as usual, dreadful, but because it was now familiar, he regretted how it faded away.

The webbing attached to his shoulder blades opened, slowing his plunge the way a parachute might. He slid down a side flue into a small fireplace on the third floor of the big old house.

Since it was midmorning, last night's fire had long since died out. The skibberee flumped into a mound of warm, soft ashes. A cloud of grey dust erupted as he landed, coating him at once.

Now, one thing about skibbereen that you'll appreciate: they are as finicky in their habits of personal hygiene as cats are. They have to be, for camouflage is their only protection. Any skibberee who is dusted with, oh, wheat flour or soot, say, shows up the color of flour or soot, every little limb and lock. Visible to the naked eye.

What-the-Dickens hated the feeling. He wanted to bathe at once. He sneezed, issuing a little crumpled fold of a sound.

"What's that?" said a voice. A croaky human voice.

He froze.

"Is that a bird fallen down the chimney?"

said the voice. "When a bird comes into a house, there's going to be a death in the family. And I know whose it is. Mine. I'm ninety-nine years old. If I could get out of bed, I'd come over there and find you, pretty little birdie, and I'd wring your pretty little neck. I'm not going to the Great Beyond till I'm ready, and I haven't seen the morning papers yet. That fool of a grandson hasn't brought me my funny pages."

What-the-Dickens had the sense that the old crackly voice wasn't really talking to him. He watched a gnarled hand emerge from some bedclothes and reach for a gnarled cane. The cane bent as it took the weight of an arm. Eventually a head emerged around the headboard.

The ancient creature peered into the fireplace.

"Can't see a cursed thing," complained the old biddy. "Left my glasses on the mantelpiece. Boy, why are you crying? Hee-hee. Get out of here, little birdie of death, before I fricassee you for lunch."

What-the-Dickens froze. If he didn't move, perhaps he wouldn't be seen.

The old woman wore a nightcap that

puffed up like a white brioche. Her sweatshirt declared, MY GRANDSON WENT TO BUSCH GARDENS AND ALL I GOT WAS THIS LOUSY SWEATSHIRT.

Guess that *wasn't the right present,* thought What-the-Dickens.

Since she'd already given to history most of her teeth, her mouth was sunken into puckers. Her face was so pleated, thought What-the-Dickens, that if you could stretch her skin until all the wrinkles were flattened out, her head would be about three feet in diameter.

A stack of books tied in a length of twine was tipped onto the floor beside her bed.

"My loved ones forget about me," she grumbled. "Birds fly into my chimney, death squats on my counterpane, and no one even brings me the newspaper. Who likes to be so alone?"

What-the-Dickens thought, *I better get out of here.*

Slowly he backed up. Every footfall raised a small cloud of dust, cloaking him further. He sneezed again once or twice, but the old woman seemed already to have forgotten about him.

Little by little What-the-Dickens found

himself foot-shelves and handholds in the spaces between the bricks lining the hearth. It wasn't hard to make his way up the flue. Every now and then he'd dislodge a clump of crumbling mortar, but in no time at all he was safely out of sight.

He came to a ledge in the chimney wall, formed where a flue from a different fireplace joined the one he'd fallen into. Here he rested a while.

I don't want to be alone, either, he thought. *But I don't want to be her pet. I want to be McCavity's pet.*

From far below bubbled the ordinary household noises: a washing machine on the rinse cycle, a radio scratchily chortling news of the tennis championships at Wimbledon. But since the skibberee could identify none of it, the house sounded full of danger.

Finally the snoring of the old woman— nap time for Granny Menace or whatever her name might turn out to be—lulled the skibberee to sleep too. He dozed all day. By the time he woke up, the blue square of sky at the top of the chimneystack had gone black, and was punctuated with stars.

The world seemed no safer than before,

but thanks to the soot, at least he was camouflaged. The appropriate dress for night was clinging to his limbs.

He summoned what courage he could muster and he continued his climb. His stomach rumbled, but not loudly enough to wake up the snoring old woman.

He would find McCavity yet. And find the right present to win her affection. He would not remain alone.

It was good to have a quest.

Rebecca Ruth sighed and rolled over. She was so busy chewing on her lamb that his nose was damp. "Tiger," she muttered in her sleep. "Tiger."

Dinah's leg had fallen asleep, but not the rest of her. She stretched out her calf, which became pestered with tingling. "Ooooh," she groaned softly, and the sound of her own fussing made her remember the fullness of their real troubles.

Hoping her voice wouldn't tremble, she said, "Knowing how hungry the skibberee is makes *me* hungry." Gingerly she got up and hobbled to the table. She was careful to spoon out only her fair share of the peaches, lying glossily in their slick of syrup. "By the way, where is all this taking place?"

"Long ago," said Gage, rejecting her offer of tuna or peach.

"I know that. You've promised you're coming into the story, and the world sounds so old-fashioned that you probably had training wheels on your two-wheeler. But I didn't ask when; I asked where. Is it around here?"

Gage rubbed his eyes.

"It was not only a decade ago," he said at last. "It was also far away. A place miles and miles upstate. A place of my childhood."

Her face fell. Gage could tell that he'd given her a disappointing answer. Dinah wanted this story local. "Can we ever go there?" she asked.

"You can't ever go back to your childhood haunts," he said, too tired to keep from sounding teacherly.

"I'm still a child," she pointed out. "*I* could go there. What's it called?"

He smiled, though the candle guttered just then and the smile, to Dinah, looked a bit like a wince. "Fern Hill," he said at last. "It was my tenth year to heaven."

"My same age," said Dinah.

Zeke twitched in his blankets. Dinah couldn't tell if he was pretending to listen to the story, or pretending not to listen. He seemed to be taking a dim view

of this story; maybe he thought he had to, with their
parents gone. He was still awake, though.

⚛ FIVE ⚛

What-the-Dickens had never seen the night
sky before. It was so vast, so salted with stars,
he got a headache. Dizzy with gaping at it, he
lost his footing and slid down the roof, ending up in a rain gutter.

Sitting up to his waist in the muck left
by yesterday's hurricane, he rubbed gritwater
out of his eyes. *I'm in an aqueduct of swamp,* he
thought, *and there—look—oh, gosh—what is
it—*

A shooting star stitched a broken line
of light across the velvet black. It was gone
before he could speak or point—but what a
jab of surprise it supplied.

He didn't know enough to say, "Star
light, star bright, first star I see tonight: I wish
I may, I wish I might, have the wish I wish
tonight."

Instead, he reached his hands up as if, by
force of devotion, he could will the brilliance
to come back.

But the shooting star didn't return. It

was oblivious to the attention of an orphan skibberee. So What-the-Dickens stood up, shook himself, and began to make his way along the gutter. Rounding the edge of a gable, he squinted through a window. Inside, he saw another glow: a plain ivory-colored night-light in a socket.

"It looks like a nice warm little tooth there, biting the dark," thought the skibberee. "*That* would make a nice present." He tried to see who was in the bed. He could make out cowboy motifs on the headboard, but he couldn't identify the lump under the covers. He only knew it wasn't old Granny Menace upstairs.

The window was closed to him. The sleeper didn't know or care about him. *Keep going,* he said to himself. *You can't catch the attention of a star; you can't wake a sleeper for company. Just keep McCavity in your heart, and find her. Offer her your allegiance. That's your job.*

At the far end of the gutter, he lost his balance. Before he could panic, his shoulder webs flared out like extra arms, stabilizing him. *Whoa!* With a little practice he found that by rotating his shoulder blades, he could stretch the webbing so it billowed like parachute silk, or relax it back into folds. Cool!

I'll show this new skill to McCavity. She'll hire me as her pet, for sure. If nothing else, my present could be to sit on her brow and keep the sun out of her sultry eyes.

What-the-Dickens took his time climbing down the side of the old house. The building had been painted ivory at some point, though now it was aging into a kind of silvery, sea-drift color. This is only important to mention because later he would need to find his way back here, and then he would be glad he had noticed a few details.

The prospect was pleasant enough. The house stood on a little rise. Several jalopies were abandoned on the back lawn, apparently being gutted for spare parts. Sheets that no amount of washing would ever get quite white again hung and flapped on clotheslines in the dark.

The world at night smells richer than it does during the day—at least for the skibbereen. They have capable noses. What-the-Dickens followed his nose and zigzagged about. McCavity, McCavity. Not anywhere near here, by the sniff of it.

He was beginning to feel practiced at things. When a field mouse darted by with a sly sideways smile, the skibberee grinned back.

I bet mice know where cats live, he thought. *Maybe I can ask for directions.*

He gave chase to the little brown creature, but he couldn't catch up fast enough to ask the question—which was lucky, for suddenly a black curse of shadow fell upon the mouse. An instant later, the squeaking mouse was airborne, clutched in the talons of an owl.

So What-the-Dickens became more wary.

He took his time and kept as hidden as he could, darting from the shadow of a trash bin to the lee of a telephone pole to the safety underneath a US mailbox. Once, by accident, he took a lift on a child's abandoned roller skate. Faster and faster it rollicked him downhill until it dumped him at a big stone gate with a sign above that read ZOO.

A curb here, a streetlight there. A gravel parking lot here, a stone wall there. What-the-Dickens tried to stay inconspicuous, but here was a piece of popcorn—yum!—and another one there, and another one beyond that. So he was learning about mealtime at last, thanks to a shuttered refreshment kiosk. The remains of spilled snacks glistened in the lamplight like edible jewels.

Caramelized peanuts. A half-melted gum-drop. Sorry, I won't talk about food anymore.

It was all pretty stale. But What-the-Dickens ate with gusto. Then he pushed beyond the snack stand. He felt braver and stronger. *McCavity,* he thought. *Am I on her trail? I can sense something.*

The popcorn led past the Elephant Palace, past the Monkey Pagoda, past the netted domes of the Tropical Bird Sanctuary, and right up to the Cat House.

What-the-Dickens smelled the big smell of big cat. McCavity? *Is this her home? Will she take me on as her pet? I'll apologize for the mama grisset's behavior. I'll make amends. I'll find her a present. She likes presents. That human said so.*

Climbing over the stone enclosure and slipping through the double rows of iron paling, What-the-Dickens readied himself to make a formal apology. He walked beneath a sign saying MAHARAJAH: BENGAL TIGER without seeing what it said.

He noticed Maharajah: a snoring mountain in the tiger keep.

Hmmm, thought What-the-Dickens, getting a closer look. *McCavity, as I recall, is more white and less orange.*

He inched forward. Now, as it happened,

Maharajah suffered from a bad toothache, and the animal surgeons were going to operate the next day. To prepare, they had fed the tiger some nice raw ribs marinated in morphine. So the tiger was having a heavier snooze than usual. Otherwise Maharajah might have felt What-the-Dickens climb up on his mighty orange-and-black foreleg, or mount the slope of his nose between his eyes.

"You're awfully big," said the skibberee. "Would you wake up and tell me where I might find a distant cousin of yours known as McCavity? You must be related: you share a common shape. She, perhaps, has let herself go, but maybe she's got big bones. I mean big bones for a small cat. Hello?"

He tugged at Maharajah's eyelid. The eye twitched open.

"Oh," said What-the-Dickens. It was a large eye, and he suddenly remembered the owl and the field mouse. A skibberee is small in any instance, and *very* small when set next to a Bengal tiger.

The tiger purred, in a kind of pain. Pain—or a persuasive lulling? You never can tell with cats. Still, What-the-Dickens thought, *Maybe I can help out a little here, in exchange for some advice.*

But how to proceed? "Is something the matter?"

Maharajah thought he was having a dream. He opened his mouth.

"Oooh." The skibberee wrinkled his nose. (Tiger breath is no joke, and there was a reek of infection.) Yet what an impressive set of choppers! "May I look in? Do you mind?" he asked politely. His eyes adjusting to the gloom, he peered. "Is that a bit of swelling on the right, there? I think it is. Shall I just nip in and see? Won't take but a moment."

For McCavity, and for her kin, he thought bravely. *Long may they smile.* Then What-the-Dickens stepped onto the tiger's tongue, which gave way spongily under his feet. He knelt down to take a better look.

The skibberee rocked the tooth in its footing. "This doesn't seem right," he said. "My gut instinct says it should come out. Shall I take care of it for you?"

Since the tiger didn't say *no,* What-the-Dickens assumed that meant *yes.* So he went to work. First he threw himself at the tooth from every direction, pushing it this way and that. Then he slid his forearm along the base of the tooth to widen the gap between the gum and the root. "Messy work, and I'll need a good cleanup when I'm done," wheezed the skibberee, "but someone's got to do it. And if you'll put in a good word for me when you next meet up with McCavity, I'd be obliged."

The jaws began to close.

"Oh, no, you don't," said the skibberee. He flexed his extended shoulder blades and he thumped the tiger in the roof of the mouth. "Open wide. Got that? We're at a delicate stage here."

A little to one side, then the other, then a little more forward. Then: Presto. The tooth was out.

A tiger tooth. It was nearly as tall as What-the-Dickens. And I am sorry to have to say it was not without blood; that's the reality of dentistry for you.

"That *is* a beauty," said the skibberee. By now, however, the pain of the extraction was getting through to the tiger. He was beginning to wake up. He began to murmur. It sounded like distant thunder at first, and then like nearer thunder. Very near. What-the-Dickens and the tooth tumbled out through the tiger's open mouth.

"Now, about McCavity—" began What-the-Dickens.

Maharajah growled, producing a gust of hot, meaty breath. What-the-Dickens was tossed aloft. He felt his shoulder limbs flail clumsily, the way the baby grissets' wings had. He was hovering three inches from the tiger's nose.

What-the-Dickens was more surprised at this than Maharajah was himself. But the skibberee pressed on. "Perhaps you can arrange for an introduction to your cousin, the white cat? And suggest a suitable present—"

The tiger roared. Still clutching the tooth, What-the-Dickens was blown backward into a trough used for tiger runoff. The skibberee sailed off down a pungent stream, through caverns measureless to man, since man can't fit in anything that small. At a clip, he bobbed along under the tiger's cage, plopping into a channel that ran out the back of the Cat House.

"Well, maybe he'll feel better in the morning," said What-the-Dickens, "though that was a lot of dirty work for no payoff. You can never be sure with cats. I guess I'm going to have to find McCavity on my own. But this thing is too heavy to carry around with me. What was I thinking? A tiger tooth is nice, but it's unwieldy as a souvenir. I suppose I could give *this* as a present to McCavity when I find her—but I have to find her, first. And I don't dare go back and interview *that* big cat."

What-the-Dickens had to act quickly. He could hear noises: the night cleaners were arriving with their broad brooms and their hoses.

He darted back to the refreshment stand, and then he saw a solution: a mousehole in the bottom of the kiosk. The field mice living inside almost had heart attacks when they noticed a tiger's tooth shoving itself in their front door.

"Sorry," said What-the-Dickens. "Do you mind terribly?"

They refused to touch it, so he guessed it would stay safe until he was ready to come back and reclaim it.

❧ ❧ ❧

There was a sound overhead.

"Thunder?" wondered Zeke. So he *was* still awake.

"It could be a jetliner flying low under the cloud," said Dinah, though since she hadn't heard a jetliner for some days, she wasn't as confident as she tried to sound. The noise seemed ominous and even brutal. But maybe it *was* a plane; and maybe it carried emergency supplies like . . . like . . . insulin, and birthday cake, and a present worthy of Rebecca Ruth, and equipment to patch up the transformer on Pilot's Knob. And maybe there were enough emergency lights to signal the plane to a safe landing.

Maybe. Maybe. Maybe there were miracles. "Is this story going to have a happy ending?" she demanded of Gage.

"Oh, who knows," he said. "I'm not there yet."

"Don't freak out, Dinah," said Zeke. "It's just a stupid fairy story. No offense, Gage. But you want to give us a story with meat, go get *The Totally Excellent Adventures of Saint Paul*. It's in my room."

"There's not enough light to read by," said Dinah huffily. "There's not nearly enough light at all. Go on, Gage. Tell us what happens next. And it better end happily."

"No promises," said Gage, as they all snuggled closer.

∾ SIX ∾

But how to locate McCavity? How could such a magnificence remain hidden? She seemed so mysterious a force—larger than life, though not larger than Maharajah.

What-the-Dickens longed to give her Maharajah's tooth. He could picture how it would happen. She would accept it, shyly tucking her furry chin into her breast. All at once, she would understand how devoted he was. She would let him be her pet, and their life together would begin. Perhaps she would wear the tooth on a string around her neck as a sign of his devotion.

Company. An end to loneliness. Bliss.

But where was she?

While he waited for inspiration—something like the shooting star, but this time something he could decipher—he might as well locate a string, too. So he could string the tiger tooth on it. Where did they keep string around here?

He thought back on his adventures since birth: the tin cabin in which he'd started his life. The appearance of McCavity and her human. The family of rust-throated grissets. The old woman in her bed—

—and then he remembered the pile of books on the floor. It had been tied with cord.

I can go back there and take a length of that, he thought.

So the skibberee made his way across the

road. Luckily, there was little nighttime traffic, so he avoided becoming roadkill.

He picked out a path through a meadow. Then he clumped up the slope of an old apple orchard let lapse into gnarly uselessness. In time — but still in the middle of the night, not the daytime yet — he got back to the ramshackle house from where he'd set out.

He stood at the base of the chimneystack and looked up all the way to the top. He felt exhausted even before he started.

Then he remembered the hovering. Could he launch himself? Could he use these flimsy attachments as wings? Could he slip the surly bonds of earth and leap tall buildings in a single bound?

He said, "Here goes nothing," really hoping it would turn out to be something.

And it did. Not something exactly elegant. It wasn't ballet in the air. But it *was* flying.

Luckily, his sense of direction was better than the mama grisset's. He achieved the old woman's windowsill and peered in. The window was open a few inches, so he stooped low and entered.

The feisty battle-ax was snoring softly. A half bottle of gin stood on the bedside table. Beside the gin bottle was a drinking glass, and in the glass a set of dentures hung suspended in water.

What-the-Dickens forgot about his hope for a piece of string. What a treasure to behold! Rank upon rank of gorgeous, full-grown pearly-browns! They were hooked and latched together somehow, a dental fringe hinged in the back and hovering slightly opened, like the smile of the Cheshire Cat without the Cat.

"I want those teeth," said What-the-Dickens.

"Eh? Whazzat?" mumbled the old woman, waking.

"The teeth," said What-the-Dickens, in transports. "May I have them?"

"I give nuzzing for nuzzing," said the old woman. Her words came out mushy and mumbly at first. "Who's speaking? Is that the voice of God? What do you want my false choppers for, God? You've already taken my real ones home to your bosom. Can't you leave me the spares?"

"I want the teeth," said What-the-Dickens.

"Give me a sign that it's God, and we'll talk," said the old woman. "I wasn't born yesterday, you know. Darn, my glasses are still on the mantelpiece. Where's that family of mine?" She took her cane and stamped it on the floor. "Hey! God is chatting me up, or some agent of heaven, but how can I tell without my specs? Someone! Yoo-hoo! Darlings! Layabouts and slugabeds! Rise and shine!"

"Shh," he said. "You'll wake them up."

"So they should *sleep* when I'm having a vision?" she snapped. "Where are you, anyway?"

What-the-Dickens hovered behind her headboard, where he could be heard but not seen. "May I have your teeth, since you've abandoned them?"

"I use them in the morning to worry my oatmeal mush to death," she replied. "Then I take them out of my mouth and scare my grandson. I'm not giving them up for love nor money. How much are you offering?"

"Money?" The skibberee didn't know about money yet, and he wasn't that sure about love, either.

"Cold hard cash. What's your best offer? Look, angel visitor, make yourself seen, or at least hand me my glasses, will you?"

What-the-Dickens fell silent. If he stayed quiet, maybe she'd fall asleep again. Then he could snatch the dentures. A *far* better present for McCavity than a tiger molar. No?

"Where'd you go?" she said suddenly. "Invisible guest, where are you?"

He stayed as still as he could.

"You've gone," she concluded, sinking back against her pillow. "Gone, gone. It was all my imagination. I was dreaming of companionship, like in the old days before I began to terrify my relatives with the force of my character. But they insist on sleeping all night long, every single night of the year, and what do they bring me for company? Nothing but books!"

She waved her cane in the air. The skibberee remembered his original goal. Looking about, he saw that the room was crowded with books. Books on the floor, books fallen under the bed, books on the mantelpiece, books on the dresser and on the seat of the rocker.

"They bring me presents. Fat comfort! *Books!* What good are books? Look at this tripe!" She lunged for a paperback volume and whipped it open, and stabbed a page with a bony finger. "'At ninety-six I had lived enough, that is all.' This is supposed to cheer up an old sinner? I don't *think* so. It's all rubbish tied with a ribbon of moonlight over the purple moor, for crying out loud."

She tossed the book aside. What-the-Dickens had to duck to avoid a concussion. "All alone, with nothing to do but read, read, read till the cows come home. And we haven't even *had* any cows around here for years, not since we sold the back acres so the feds could put up that blasted highway cloverleaf." She honked into a handkerchief. Her weeping was silly but her sorrow was real.

What-the-Dickens took advantage of her distress. Could he could get those dentures yet?

He trilled his wings and settled on the night table. While her shoulders were turned, he grabbed at the mighty teeth by their sticky artificial gums.

He was enthralled. Oh, what a jackpot!

"Gotcha," she said, and snatched the teeth away from him with one hand, while she up-ended the glass of stinky water right over him with the other. "Oh, what a jackpot!"

Caged in a glass cylinder, and his wings too drenched even to flap. How embarrassing. How wet.

"I *knew* you were still around some-where," she said. She fit the teeth into her mouth. They seemed too big for her face and they broadened her smile into a leer. "So. The Angel of Death comes in on little cat feet, eh? Well, I'm gunning for a hundred and I've got some months to go yet. So listen up. I'm not leaving this vale of tears till I've had my cake and my birthday wish. And a decent present would be a welcome bonus. *Anything but books.*"

He couldn't breathe. He pounded against the glass.

"Frantic little busybody, ain't you?" she observed. She came close and her eyes, through the glass, were damp and milky and smart. "Somehow I thought they'd send somebody a bit more senior to carry me off. Well, not my problem. What're you buzzing about in there for, fellow?"

"Let me out," he said. "You've made a mistake. Or I've made a mistake. This is a mistake." But could she hear him? He was behind glass, and she seemed deaf to his pleas.

"I am so lonely up here with nothing but *books.* You can be my *pet,*" she said decisively. She tapped a crooked finger with a long ragged nail against the side of the tumbler.

"Please," he said. "I thought I wanted to be a pet. But I don't. I can't breathe in here."

He lurched this way and that, his webwings smacking the glass, his feet kicking at it. "Let me out. I don't want your teeth anymore. I'll leave you your string. Let me go. Please, old lady—please!"

"Stop fluttering so—you're making me seasick. Maybe you're bored?" she asked. "Here's a book. I'll put it next to you. I'll turn pages on this book once a day. It's only 567 pages. You'll be occupied, and I'll reach a hundred and the president will write me a letter."

Her fingers fumbled, grabbing the crinkly cellophane slipcover over a hardcover volume from the public library. "The little ones will like to see this gorgeous moth," she said, more to herself than to the skibberee. For a moment her voice was less theatrical, more internal. "I'll call them up to see my catch, and they'll come to visit their granny at last. What a stroke of luck for me! I'm too old and dull for them, but now I have this huge lovely insect as bait. I'll tell them it was a present from Mother Nature. Maybe they'll stay a while and keep me company. A moth who reads! Little ones will believe anything."

She opened the book to the title page. *One Hundred Years of Solitude*. She stood the book open, two angled walls of white pages kept from riffling shut by the water glass set between them.

He backed away in horror. Since there was water on the nightstand, the drinking glass slid a quarter inch on its slickness.

Aha.

In just a moment, What-the-Dickens managed to push the drinking glass more than an inch off the rim of the bedside table. Hidden from her prying eyes by the opened novel, What-the-Dickens popped out of the overturned glass like a rabbit sneaking out of the false bottom of a magician's hat.

He left her there, still giddy with glee at having trapped either the Fairy of Death or an oversized moth. He left her teeth there. He left the twine there.

What-the-Dickens reached the fresh air. He had no present for McCavity, but at least he'd escaped becoming a present himself.

"Fairy of Death!" Zeke's tone was withering. "This is getting seriously bizarre. I don't think our parents would approve. We're supposed to govern ourselves, not go to pieces. Do you really believe this nonsense?"

"I'm telling a story," said Gage, taking no offense.

"In this household," said Zeke, "we believe only in what is real."

"The storm is real," said Gage, "and comfort is real, too. The existence of stories is real. Your hero told parables all the time; you know that."

Zeke reared up on one elbow, ready for battle. "The devil can quote scripture for his own purpose."

"Any louder, you two, and you'll wake the baby," said Dinah. "And I have a headache. Could you both be charitable and, like, shut up?"

Kindly, they did.

It wasn't a headache she had, though. It was a memory, a sudden one, of her mother and father talking about some of this same stuff a few weeks earlier.

"Dinah, your runaway imagination," said her mother. "'First star I see tonight, I wish I may, I wish I might'? I don't think so. Wishes are for play. Prayers are for real."

"I know what's real," said Dinah.

"You can't trust in wishes. You trust in God. It's harder to do, but worth it. You become a better person."

"You want me perfect," said Dinah. "I get so

perfect, then I'm perfectly—lonely. Too good to have friends."

Her mother corrected her. "I don't want you perfect. I want you Dinah. The best Dinah you can be. Belief in God doesn't make you better than anyone else—but with luck, it might make you better than you would otherwise be."

"With luck?"

Her dad, in the other room, had laughed warmly. "She got you there, darlin'."

Her mom had replied, "With grace. Have a good mind, honey, but don't be a clever weasel."

Dinah heard this all again in the dark, as if her parents were right there with her, hovering, shadow-like and indistinct, protecting her. But what if they were dead by now, and Dinah's memory was of their ghosts, passing by, blessing her for a last time?

Gage was saying to Zeke, in a peacemaking tone, "Belief in something, anything, may or may not make you a better person, Zeke—depending on what the belief is—but it can make you different. You listen to a story together, though, and your differences can dissolve a little. Isn't that okay? For a while? In an emergency?"

Zeke didn't answer, but turned his spine away from the others.

SEVEN

What-the-Dickens tried to think things through. To add things up. (Skibbereen have a hard time at this; the best that the smartest of them can do with adding two plus two is guessing: three plus one. Correct, sort of, but not always useful.)

In his first day of life, he'd gained very little and he'd lost his ambition to become a pet to McCavity. He'd based his hopes on a sorry notion, if being a pet meant prison. Suffocation. Slavery.

So he was out in the wind, out in the wild, with nothing but his drying wings and his loneliness to believe in. And even though he lacked a grasp of basic math, he realized that this didn't seem to add up to much.

Without a destination, What-the-Dickens flew the way the mama grisset might have done—this way and that, meandering like a butterfly or a bee. A butterfly or a bee in panic mode. He touched down; he lifted off. He looked and then he closed his eyes.

He was not so much aloft as adrift.

He ought to have slept, you know. Sleep is good for anyone in distress. But he couldn't.

He bumbled left, right, up, and down. Like a moth, occasionally he was drawn to the light in some isolated window, but he grew too scared to come closer in case he became trapped again.

The mama grisset has her young, he thought. *Maharajah and McCavity are clearly cousins of some sort. Even the shriveled crone in the attic seems to have her family downstairs. Whom do I have of my own? Nobody.*

In his terror at this sudden clarity, he entered the hot airspace over the chimney flue of a baker who, in the ancient tradition of bakers, had risen early to knead the dough for the day's loaves. What-the-Dickens tumbled in the thermal, heel over head and wing tips over heels. The heat made him pass out, but his wings didn't entirely forget their new talent. Instinct told his wings to break the speed of his fall to earth, and his wings obeyed.

Still, when he fell at last, he was winded, wounded of limb, and shattered of spirit. Crumpled upon himself, he rolled to a stop against the back wheel of the bakery's delivery truck.

GOODNESS BAKERY
THE BEST BAKED GOODS

said the truck, black and gold letters on a red background, though What-the-Dickens was beyond reading anything.

Like it or not, he slept.

And so should I. And so should you. Do you hear me?

MIDNIGHT

"A GOOD PLACE TO TAKE A BREAK," said Gage. "We really should get some sleep. We're not doing ourselves a favor sitting up all night, believe me."

They stood and stretched. Gage cracked his knuckles. First Dinah, then Zeke went to have a pee. Having already taken care of her pee while she cuddled in blankets, Rebecca Ruth slept on.

The man and the two older children gathered in the breezeway to study the weather. Dinah wondered if the storm was losing some strength. The air seemed to move with a more stately progress than before—didn't it? Or was that wishful thinking on her part?

In a kind of slow-motion anguish, the trees tossed their heads. The sound of ten million leaves palming against each other. The sound of deep night.

"Sounds like a laugh track playing very far away," said Gage.

"We don't do laugh tracks, not in this house," Dinah reminded her cousin. "No TV. Besides, who could be laughing at a time like this?"

"Choirs of angels might," suggested Zeke. "They know it will come out all right."

"Even if they knew the future, why should they laugh?" Dinah shot back. "Laugh at our misery now?"

"Oh, answer your own question, if my answer doesn't suit you," said Zeke. "I suppose you think the wind sounds more like — like some sort of campfire songfest, with crowds of Juliettes and Brittneys swaying back and forth, going 'The worms crawl in, the worms crawl out,' and on and on."

"Ezekiel Hiram Jehosophat Ormsby," began Dinah in a murderous tone.

"I was going to go try the generator again," said Gage, "but I hate to leave you here squabbling."

"I'll come help," said Dinah, wanting to get away from her brother for a spell. "Zeke can mind the baby."

"I'm the boy. I'll help Gage," said Zeke. "Mind Rebecca Ruth yourself."

Gage had had enough. He left them both behind. "Chew each other up all you want," he told them.

"Just give us a break here, will you? Don't wake your sister. Please? It took long enough for her to settle."

Zeke promised nothing; so Dinah wouldn't either. Seething silently, they cupped their hands to peer through the window, watching Gage with a lackluster flashlight. He flipped switches; he fiddled with wires. He peered at directions printed on the side of the housing, running his hands to sluice off the rain-smear so he could decipher the engineering language. But the secrets of a gas-powered generator remained beyond him.

Dinah sympathized. There was so much of the world that she, too, couldn't figure out. Or even imagine. Like where her friends Brittney and Juliette might be tonight. Where in the whole world. Or why they, wherever the blazes they were, should have the comfort of their parents, and Dinah only had—

"I like Gage," she heard herself say, in the wrong tone, brutally.

"Useless," agreed Zeke.

"He's not useless."

"He wouldn't be useless if only he'd be right once in a while. I should have gone scavenging for supplies today, and you know it."

"You didn't, though," she snapped. "At least when I had a plan, I carried it out. I went downslope to give blessings and hugs to Juliette and Brittney. I didn't just talk about it."

"Yeah, and you'd have gotten in a heap of trouble if everything hadn't gotten so out of control—" said Zeke, but this brought the subject of their parents too close. The sudden panic, the medical questions, their mother's tears, the quick prayer consultation in the driveway, the departure, as the echoes of distant thunder shuddered down the hills again. . . .

Remembering this, Dinah wanted to reach out and hold Zeke's hand, just for a moment, but he was a jerk, so she didn't.

When he returned, Gage looked so dejected that Dinah said, not as convincingly as she would have liked, "Don't worry, Gage. It's probably for the best. If you'd gotten the contraption working, the lights would've all gone on and woken up Rebecca Ruth. Maybe tomorrow someone will come along and fix it for us. That's time enough."

"Huh," said Zeke, noncommittally.

"Besides," said Dinah, "whatever food was left in the fridge has rotted already. So we don't really need a working fridge."

"We have to get some milk for the birthday girl sooner or later," said Gage, "and we're going to need to refrigerate it."

"Maybe tomorrow will be the time to leave," said Zeke, as they returned to the front room on tiptoe. His expression said, We all know that yesterday was the time to leave.

Dinah looked at Gage, to see if he would say, No, the time is past; we can't get out anymore. But he said nothing for a long time.

"Are you going to sleep?" asked Dinah in a softer voice.

Again, quiet, for so long that the children were sure the answer must be yes. But then Gage opened his eyes and winked. "Just tricking you to see if you'd nod off a little. I mean if I did."

"You can sleep," said Zeke. "Be my guest. I'm on duty. I'll keep watch. It's our house, anyway."

"Oh no, he can't sleep," protested Dinah. "I want to know about What-the-Dickens."

"He can tell us tomorrow. His . . ."— Zeke edited his opinions midsentence—". . . little story will keep."

"Tomorrow," said Dinah, "we'll have fresh worries to bother us, Zeke."

"Is there anyone else out there?" asked Zeke. "I mean, if the time has come to leave, who will we find out there?"

Dinah clutched her knees. That's what she worried about, too. That even the looters might have moved on. Moved out. Gotten out while they could.

Gotten out if they could.

She jabbed Gage under the ribs. "Where are we?" she said in a chattery whisper, to keep herself from flying apart.

Gage pulled himself upright again and rubbed both his eyes with the heels of his hands. "I'd rather talk than sleep," said Gage. That remark is a fiction, thought Dinah. By the hooded look in her brother's eyes, she guessed that Zeke thought Gage's remark an out-and-out lie.

Neither of them spoke, though. They just waited, expectantly, in the dark, for the engine of storytelling to turn over and start up again—to do the thing that the blasted generator refused to do—to keep them warm throughout the night.

HIDDEN FORBIDDEN

❧ EIGHT ❧

As the baker stacked his morning loaves and cakes on his truck, What-the-Dickens snored on. He slept until the baker turned the key in the truck's ignition and the engine puttered to life and backfired. The explosion jolted the skibbereee to his senses.

Before he had time to react, the truck pulled away.

GOODNESS BAKERY, said the shiny letters on the side of the truck as it careered away.

"Well, thank goodness," murmured What-the-Dickens, glad not to have been pulverized. But as he awakened further, the reality of his situation fell heavily upon him. He remembered with shame his quest to find McCavity and give her a gift, and apply for a job as her pet. What a silly dream all of that had been.

He was older now, and wiser. He was a day and a half old. He had to face the facts of his solitude.

He had to find a life, or make one up from scratch.

What-the-Dickens stood and rubbed his thimble-hips. The day was starting out good, and not so good. He hadn't been crushed by a bakery truck, true — but the same truck was barreling away too fast for him to follow, taking with it the sweet scent of warm cinnamon rolls and raspberry jam coffee cakes.

Though the sky was still dark, a paler grey bleared the eastern horizon. Night was hurrying toward morning at the rate of — is it? — a little more than a thousand miles an hour. But there was still a half hour before dawn.

The dew that had settled on the ground had settled on the skibberee, too. It made his limbs stiff. He stood and shivered for a while, and then he launched himself. "But where to?" he murmured, trying not to think of McCavity. "One hundred years of solitude, here I come."

He flew as much to warm up as to travel. He wasn't particularly zippy as a pilot, he discovered. His big feet hung down. Hovering a foot or two above the ground, he meandered like a big old bee bumbling his way home after an afternoon spent hitting the nectar.

At length the skibberee came across a children's swing set, all rusting poles and creaking chains, and a weathered wooden seesaw, and a slide that went only down. The wind set the swings moving faintly. Among the exposed roots of a lilac hedge nosed an abandoned plastic ball, a sad clown face printed on it.

What-the-Dickens didn't know what a playground was, but he could recognize its emptiness.

He sat on the swing. The size of a hamster in height, and of a clothespin in girth, he couldn't move the swing on his own, even when he powered up his wings. When the wind stopped, the swing stopped too.

He tried the seesaw, but as everyone

knows, a seesaw is no fun unless there are two of you. It just doesn't work.

Finally What-the-Dickens flew to the top of the slide. To someone his size, it looked like a Matterhorn made out of titanium. He sat down and slalomed down the slope of it, ending up face-first in the mud at its base. "My life," he mumbled to himself, a mouth full of grit. "Going nowhere fast."

Then he found a board on which to balance. The edge of a sandbox, an old-fashioned one with wooden sides, held back sand packed like brown sugar and damp with dew.

In the middle of the nearest dune, What-the-Dickens spotted a footprint in the sand.

"Hello," he said to the footprint, foolishly.

He couldn't help it, though. This was a footprint of someone his own size, though someone with a narrower instep, a daintier tread than his. The footprint was pointing toward a second, about an inch or so beyond; and a third, and a fourth.

The little track went to the top of the low-lying dune—What-the-Dickens traced it—and then it disappeared. It just stopped in midtrek.

Who could it be? *Is it a sign of that si-lent fellow with whom I once shared lodgings in an empty can?* he wondered. Maybe it was another mouse who had gotten carried away by an owl, and that's why the path stopped mid-dune. Or could it be a bird, like the mama grisset, who landed in the sand, hunted for worms, and then skittered up the slope and flew off again?

The world, though lonely, wasn't entirely unpeopled. It felt good to remember this. It felt good to feel good.

What-the-Dickens looked around. Beyond the playground crouched a long, low build-ing with automobiles parked in front. It was an old-fashioned motel—a motor court—though What-the-Dickens didn't grasp the concept.

This was in the country, remember, and it wasn't an especially prosperous neck of the woods. Air-conditioning was supplied by nature. So most of the windows of the bed-rooms were opened for a little air.

In one of the window screens he discov-ered a useful slit, several inches high. Its edges were folded back. It was perfect for slipping through. So he did.

NINE

It took a moment for his eyes to adjust to the gloom.

A pair of beds. In one, a grown-up snored underneath a forearm thrown across the face. In the other, a child breathed soundlessly. The bathroom light had been left on, and the door was open a few inches, so in a moment the room swam into focus.

Next to the adult's bed was a magazine; the grown-up had been reading before sleep. (What-the-Dickens looked to see if there was a spare smile of teeth in a glass, but no such luck: only a ticking alarm clock.) On the child's side of the table flopped an open coloring book and three rubbed-down crayons.

What-the-Dickens flew closer. He was drawn to the coloring book. It showed scenes from *Peter Pan*. I don't know which, maybe the Disney version—I only heard about this later. Anyway, the page was opened to a drawing of Tinker Bell. Busty, pouty, peeved, and, the way she was dressed, in danger of catching a serious cold. She had wings, though to What-the-Dickens's eye they appeared inadequate to the task of hoisting her aloft. She looked as if she might be suffering from some lower back strain.

"Wow," said What-the-Dickens. He looked closer. "Wow."

"Are you out of your cotton-picking mind?"

He whipped around, half expecting to find Tinker Bell in the flesh. Instead, he came face to face with an enraged little firecracker of a creature. She was hovering off the bed-side table with her own set of wings set on *ratchet*.

His heart wanted to lift up—society! Someone he could talk to!—but she looked pretty steamed.

"What the dickens—" she said in a whisper that was more like a hiss.

She knows my name. Extraordinary. But how? "That's me," he said.

"What do you think you're doing in here?"

"I don't think—"

"Well, *that* much is obvious!" She waved her arms. "Lower your voice and dim your headlights, you nincompoop. You got no sense at all?"

"I doubt it." *At least my answer is honest,* he thought. *Maybe she'll lighten up.* "Do you?"

He looked her up and down to see if she might appear to have sense. She looked much like himself, only her sheer wings were yellow and pale purple, whereas his — he noticed for the first time — were a sort of turquoise blue. She sported a backpack of some sort.

"Who are you?" he asked, and added, "And, if I'm not being too forward, *what* are you?"

"I'm Pepper," she said, "and if you can't tell I'm a girl, you're an even bigger loser than you look like. I'm a—" But she stopped herself. "You don't get that information out of me, you spy. You interloper. Get lost, before I call in reinforcements."

"I mean, what sort are you? What tribe? What variety? I'm What-the-Dickens," he continued. "That's what my name is. But beyond that, I'm afraid, I don't know much else about myself. And even less about you."

"Now look. I don't care if your name is Saint Wisdom Tooth. This is our territory, buster," she said. "And it's my job, and I got to do it right. Don't try to horn in where you ain't wanted. I'm doing a simple snatch-'n'-scram. In and out, no muss, no fuss. Giving you the benefit of the doubt, you're on the wrong job site, you. Worst case scenario, you're an enemy agent pretending to be a moron. Now get lost before I beat you up."

He had the sense she was talking big, and that she was alarmed. He didn't know he could alarm anyone, and the feeling was weird but not entirely objectionable. "I have no idea what you're yammering about, and that's the truth," he said.

"Who *are* you?" she asked.

Well, that was the question, wasn't it? He hardly knew. "What-the-Dickens," he reminded her.

She put a finger to her lips, signifying *Hush,* and she beckoned him to follow her.

They flew into the small bathroom adjacent to the bedroom. It smelled of disobedient drains. A fluorescent light flickered bluely across a sink set in a Formica countertop. A spill of baby powder, a bottle of aspirin, two old splayed-bristle toothbrushes. Pepper screeched in for a landing on the baby powder, which afforded her some increased friction and drag. What-the-Dickens, less schooled in such maneuvers, tried the same move, but he smacked his new associate into one of the toothbrushes.

"Ow!" She righted herself. "Fly often, do we? Clumsy oaf."

"Sorry."

"Now listen up, you. I'm giving you a chance to back off and disappear. No questions asked. Maybe you're some extra-dim lowlife element horning in on my route. Or maybe you're an advance party scout from some other dumb tribe. Either way, if you don't vamoose, you can prepare to meet your maker. I didn't come this far just to lose my license because of some two-bit tooth thief." She grabbed one of the toothbrushes and held it before her horizontally, like a pike staff. "Get in my way, silly boy, and you're going to have the proverbial Brush with Death."

"Put that down—you'll hurt someone," he said. "What *are* you snapping at me about?"

She eyed the other toothbrush. *Is she expecting me to grab it and fight with her? I won't.*

Perhaps his just standing there, neither aggressive nor defensive, persuaded her to relax a little.

"Teeth," she said. "My information says Claire Dahl. Mandibular central incisor. This is our territory, and this is my beat. You forgotten we don't work in pairs? Get your wings checked, why don't you? Or I'll report to headquarters—"

"My wings are fine," he said, shivering them in emphasis. "And I'm not spying for anyone. I've got no one to spy for."

"Right," she replied sourly. "So what are you doing here, then? Have you botched up your own assignment? Your wings are giving off nutso readings, buster."

His shoulders drooped. He said, "I don't know what you're talking about. The wings *are* tingling somewhat. Are they malfunctioning?"

"Don't you know how they work?"

He shook his head.

"You're *that* new on the job?" She peered a little closer. "Are you one of us, and I just never met you? What, they sent me a trainee without telling me? That's rich, even for them. No, I don't believe it. I'm a solo operator. I don't do *teamwork*."

"I don't know where I am. I don't know what the job is. I don't know why my wings are tingling." But he was excited: he was about to find out.

Pepper dropped the toothbrush. "Oooh, is the little fellow dim, or what? Stupid boys are the cutest. Look," she continued. She arched her back and her wings rose and opened. Small beads of light ran frantically from stem to stern. "The wings of skibbereen ain't just *fashion accessories,* you know."

"Skibbereen?" It was the first time he'd heard the term.

"And they're not just for flying," she continued. "Wings are part of the colony's central communication system. Through your wings you pick up your assignments, your updates. The daily buzz. That sort of thing. The tingling you're talking about? Unless you've got some sort of bug, you're just raking in the data from headquarters. Didn't no one clue you in?"

He said, "I'm an orphan, I think. I never met anyone else before you." He didn't know about shaking hands, but he held out both his hands in a rush of enthusiasm, as if to grab her own hands and—twist them, or kiss them, or something. He couldn't tell what he was supposed to do, but he could feel he was supposed to do *something.*

She shoved her hands in her pockets. "Well, that beats all," she said. "It really does. But I got no time to conduct a private seminar for you. I got a tooth to retrieve. Duty calls. Neither snow nor rain nor sleet nor gloom of night, they say, though the wind slowed me down some, and morning will be here shortly.

You want to watch, learn the ropes—I can't like it, but I can't stop you. But a skibberee can't be seen. It's not allowed."

"Be seen by what?" He was spastic with curiosity.

She put her fingers to her lips. "Sweet *tooth*! Will you *hush*? Sometimes I wonder why I ever went into this line of work. Then I remember. The other options stink."

"I can help," said What-the-Dickens. "Can't I?"

Pepper looked at him with half-lowered eyelids. "I told you. Your help is exactly what I don't need. So thanks in advance for nothing, and I really mean that."

"Oh, look!" he said. In the bathroom mirror that was mounted above a backsplash panel over the sink and counter, What-the-Dickens had caught sight of a forehead. He recognized the familiar high-arched eyebrows (his friend from the tin can had appeared permanently astonished) and the ill-kept weedy hair. "He's back," he said. "There he is. I knew he wouldn't abandon me forever."

"Lower your voice and keep your eyes down," snapped Pepper. "Where *have* you been? We don't do mirrors. Skibbereen are never seen, not even by ourselves."

"Mirrors?" he said.

"Oooh, so we start from scratch. The baby pool. Look, What-the-Chicken, that fellow is a reflection," she said, "not a twin. We all have them if we stumble accidentally in front of a mirror. I have one too." She waved at hers and it waved back, but What-the-Dickens noticed they kept their eyes closed—both Pepper and her identical twin. "It's not real. You can't believe in it as a sidekick. See?"

He saw, but he didn't quite see, yet.

From her shoulder she loosened a coil of slender white filament. "A skibberee's best friend," she said. She tied a wide noose into the cord and began to twirl it. In a moment it was going over her head, and she was leaping back and forth through it.

"Amazing," said What-the-Dickens, entranced. She could do all this with her eyes shut. Was there no end to her talent?

"Look at the mirror," she panted. He saw that her reflection was doing the same thing that she was—exactly, exactly. And it stopped when she stopped.

"It's a picture of something, of us," she said. "That's all. It isn't real."

He'd have felt more devastated if he'd been alone, but at least he had Pepper to explain it to him. "You're good," he said.

"Made the quarterly finals in my division last season," she said, winding up the cord again and slinging it back over her shoulder. "And now it's to work. If you're not a spy and you're not a last-minute apprentice, I'll leave you to your business, and I'll take care of mine." She lowered her brow and her wing spangles dimmed, and before he knew it, she had launched herself from the bathroom counter.

He had no other plans for the rest of his life. He followed her.

She zipped to the doorway, but she paused in midair and waited for him to catch up. In a voice as faint as dust, she mouthed, "Now remember. No butting in. I need this one for my record, bad."

He looked again at the beds. The small human was a girl, sweet in her sleep—smelling like warm gingersnaps. Her head had fallen down the slope of pillow, rucking up one corner of it.

On the flowery sheet beneath the corner of the pillow, a single pearly tooth lay exposed.

"It's all in the timing," whispered Pepper. "Hang back, kiddo, and watch a pro at work."

She arose an inch or two higher to launch into a dive, and What-the-Dickens twiddled his fingers in curiosity.

If his flying was like that of an airborne toad, Pepper's was more like the dance of a hummingbird. In the glowing blue of the predawn room, Pepper glowed a complementary mauve. She looked no more substantial than the exhalation of breath from a sleeping child.

She made landfall on the cresting seam of the pillow and lightly ran along its ridgetop. Then, using her wings as baffles to slow her descent, she slid down the steep cotton cliffside and approached the tooth.

What-the-Dickens remembered his risky encounter with Maharajah and thought, *Is Pepper going to perform dental surgery on that poor sleeping creature? She oughtn't—so many dreadful things could happen.*

The child snuffled and rolled over a little. The pillow lowered upon the tooth, covering it.

Pepper wasn't fussed. From her shoulder she unhitched the coil of white thread. Once she got it twirling, she sent the looped end sailing toward the top corner of the pillow. She lassoed the peak of the pillow and pulled tightly on the cord. Then, when the knot was secure, she flew backward so she could sling the cord around the bedpost.

He was slack-jawed with admiration. She was able to use the cord and the bedpost as a pivot and hoist. Hand over little hand she pulled on the cord, and the pillow slowly lifted in the air, revealing the hidden tooth.

Should I grab it? he wondered. But Pepper had told him to stay well out of it, and in deference to his new friend, he decided to obey her.

She worried the tooth forward with her foot, and then she gripped the cord in her mouth. Both hands now free, she opened the flap of the knapsack she wore on her back. She extracted something, a silvery disc of some sort, worked over with symbols and numbers and letters. Pepper slid this under the pillow where the tooth had been. Hand under hand, she returned the pillow to its supine position.

A magnificent showing. *A triumph,* he thought.

Then he stuffed his fist in his mouth to keep from crying out. The alarm clock on the bedside table had started to hop and jangle like a box full of killer bees.

Pepper did not hesitate. She deposited the

tooth in her satchel and flew up to loosen the noose of the white cord.

The child flumped over, undisturbed, but the adult opened her eyes and groaned. "Shoot me now. It can't be morning already," she mumbled. "What time is it anyway?"

She felt for the alarm clock, which was shrilling away. "Where are you, you blasted nuisance."

What-the-Dickens thought, *All is lost!*

He dove forward, barreling against the alarm clock, knocking it right off the tabletop. A crash on the floor. The girl sat up suddenly. "I'll get up!" she barked. "You don't have to throw things around the room!"

"Sorry, Claire," said the grown-up. "Did I do that? Are you all right?"

Pepper had alighted on the headboard of the little girl's bed. She jerked her head toward the window, meaning, *Outta here, fellow, while we still can.* She zipped across the room just as the grown-up finally got her fingers on the light switch. What-the-Dickens followed Pepper through the hole in the screen.

"That was close," he panted. "You could've been killed in there."

"Piece of cake," she said smugly, though he thought she was a bit rattled. "However, if I hadn't wasted so much time giving you the lowdown, I'd have been in and out of there like nobody's business. The alarm clock would not have been an issue."

"I saved your life," he said. "Did I, do you think?"

"You endangered it. You were stupider even than you look," she replied. "You shoulda stayed out of it like I said. Skibbereen are never seen. That's the first thing you learn in nursery camp."

"I see you," he said.

"Skibbereen are never seen *by humans*. Didn't your mother ever teach you anything?"

He didn't answer.

"Come on, it's getting light. It'll be dawn in a jiffy. We better get undercover before anyone sees us. Follow me," she said.

"Where are we going?" he asked.

"Second star to the right, and straight on till morning coffee," she snapped.

"It looks like morning already."

"Better not be, or I'm fried. Come on, we're going to go home, clock off, and get some breakfast. Shut up and fly."

Home, thought What-the-Dickens. *Home?*

He could guess at what the word meant,

but not to whom it belonged. Pepper, probably. Not him. How could it belong to him?

❧ TEN ❧

Pepper had a head start on him. What-the-
Dickens struggled to keep from losing sight
of her. He could summon no extra breath for
screeching out questions.

Still, he managed to look and see how
Pepper could move so fast. She used her wings
in a cunning way. First she flapped furiously
to activate liftoff and reach her desired eleva-
tion. Then she settled the ball of her leading
foot upon the ankle of the following foot, so
that the knee of the forward leg broke the air.
This gave her the look of an old-fashioned
hood ornament on a car, or a figurehead on a
sailing ship.

What-the-Dickens tried to imitate the
form. Ha! With his clodhopper feet like lima
beans, he flattened and slowed his progress
rather than speeding it up. Still, it was good
to experiment. He tried kneeling in the air,
resting his feet against his little bum. He
improved a little.

He paid so much attention to his ath-
letic form that he didn't think to mark his

progress above the landscape. He was largely unaware of the gentle swells of hill, the nubble of shadowy forest, and the raked lines of plowed fields. Nor of the buildup of traffic on the roads as the sun came close to breaking over the horizon.

Pepper angled her wings for a descent, and she changed the stance of her legs. She made a sudden drop toward a stand of scrub grass and overgrown junk trees choking a patch of land encircled by a highway cloverleaf ramp. The orphan skibberee followed her lead and did the same.

He had to work not to close his eyes while plummeting through the fringed flats of green leaves. Leveling, he saw beneath him a neatly sawed-off tree trunk. Lightning bugs of some sort, trained for the job no doubt, stood all around the edge of the trunk in parallel lines, beaconing the travelers safely in.

Pepper landed in the center, gracefully enough. Then What-the-Dickens smacked her off balance as he thudded into her. "Whoops," he said. "That's twice in one day. Sorry."

Several dozen wingless skibbereen came rushing forward to link arms and make a living guardrail, saving Pepper from plunging off the edge of the tree trunk like a fighter pilot overshooting on the deck of an aircraft carrier. But they laughed as they did it, without particular affection.

"Look who's back," they chortled. "She's a stitch, she is. And look what the cat dragged in. *He's* a bit of a rube, ain't he? Your basic bran muffin without a full portion of raisins."

"Mind your manners," said Pepper, "or I'll clock you." She shucked off the shoulder bag holding the tooth and she began to swing it around. The welcoming committee backed off a little.

"Oooh, spitfire mama," they said. They all seemed to say the same words more or less at the same time—they were like a second-grade class reciting a familiar poem: some too fast, some slow, but more or less on the same line. "Pepper's here, Pepper's here, someone kick her in the rear." Then one began to call, and the others to echo, "Stump mistress! Stump mistress! We have a foreign body!"

An older skibberee, rather fuller in the waistline than the rest of them, rushed forward. What-the-Dickens straightened up and grinned at her. She was shaped more like a mouse than a grasshopper. "Lord love a duck," she wheezed, "what you got for Old Flossie then?"

"A mandibular central incisor from a human, name of Claire Dahl. A visitor to these parts," reported Pepper.

"I mean the skibberee flotsam," said Old Flossie.

"I thought you'd know," said Pepper. "Didn't you send him to slow me down and complicate my exam?"

"Did not," said Old Flossie. "He's a spy."

"He's not a spy," said Pepper. "He's too stupid to be a spy."

"That's right," said What-the-Dickens helpfully. "I wouldn't even know what I was spying to find out."

"Hmmm." The older skibberee cast a sideways glance at the tooth Pepper was unpacking from her satchel. "Oooh, that's a lovely specimen, that is. But Pepper, my chickadee, you're late."

Pepper shrugged as if she didn't care, but Old Flossie puckered her brow. "Now don't get above your station, young lady. None of this modern snippety-uppity stuff with me—I won't have it. You know the rules. You're to be in before sunrise with your cargo.

You're a few moments late. Aren't you still on probation pending your license review? I think you are."

"I told you. I was detained," said Pepper. "I got waylaid by this bozo."

There was a gasp. "You didn't take him along on your campaign and . . . and . . . collaborate with him, whoever he is?" Old Flossie frowned harder. "That's entirely forbidden. This could cost you merit marks, missy."

"Of course I didn't take him along. You think I'm a fool?"

Old Flossie glowered as if the jury was still out on that question, but made a motion with her finger: *Go on.*

"He intercepted me as I was about to start. He delayed me. He seems harmless, though he don't know the rules. I couldn't just abandon him there. Leave him behind to be discovered. *Skibbereen are never seen,* and so on? All that nursery school training? So I had no choice but to bring him back with me. That's why I'm late. Frankly, I figured I'd get some extra credit for handling the situation well." She seemed both peeved and a little worried.

"I am afraid Doctor Ill will not look kindly on any of this," said Old Flossie, sniffing. She poked at the tooth with a blackened fingernail. What-the-Dickens thought, *Did Pepper bring this as a present? Old Flossie doesn't seem too grateful. Or impressed.*

"Hmm," said the stump mistress, frowning. "Some tartar buildup. Well, we'll clean it up and see what happens. Come on, you thingy. You don't fool me. Where's your colony? What's your name? Out with it."

"What-the-Dickens," he said. "Are you my mother?"

"Now isn't that the stupidest old thing to say," she groused. "Do I look like anyone's mother?"

"I wouldn't know. I never met a skibberee mother before."

"Well, you haven't now, either," she said. "Where do you hail from, Dickens?"

"I was born a couple of days ago."

"Not of *our* stock. Where's your tribe gotten to, and why are you apart from them? Banished? Abandoned? Or did you stop to do your business and no one noticed when you got left behind?"

The other skibbereen on the stump laughed so hard they began to glow red and blow gummy clots out of their noses.

"I don't know. I don't really understand

how creatures get born, or what a tribe means. Or even what I am, if it comes right down to it. Or what you are."

"Me? Old Flossie? I'm a professional shrew." She laughed in a manner not altogether kindly, but not menacingly, either. "You're in luck, though; tonight's the monthly Duty Pageant, and that's an earful and an eyeful, and it'll stuff you with civic pride. Just mark my words." She sniffed. "Is that tuna on your breath?"

"It's tuna on my wings, I think."

"You need a good bath. I'll show you where. Let's go."

What-the-Dickens glanced at his new associate. Pepper seemed somewhat unsure of herself.

"Come with me," he said to her.

"No, she can't," interrupted Old Flossie. "She has to get this tooth down to Central Supply so it can be registered on the manifest. Don't detain her. She hasn't got the best record among the training Agents. As for you, you'll be needing an interview with Doctor Ill. But let's get you a bath so you're presentable. Look smart, now; here's the doorway."

When the stump mistress led What-the-Dickens past them, the other skibbereen fell back as if afraid of toxic contagion. He turned to look at Pepper, but she was being hustled away by a crowd of chattering skibbereen. They blathered, "You could've been killed! He might've done you in! You're lucky to be alive! That's some tooth you snatched!"

The plump old skibbereen shifted aside a pumpkin-colored fungus that grew on the edge of the stump. Behind the growth appeared a round hole. Old Flossie could barely squeeze in, but squeeze in she did, at last, descending a staircase into the interior of the tree trunk.

What-the-Dickens looked back one more time. Pepper had paused on the other edge of the stump, resisting the surge of the crowd escorting her away. What-the-Dickens raised his eyebrows: *Should I?*

She shrugged back at him: *What do I care?* But she must care about something, for she looked more than a little worried. She finally made a motion to him— *Go, go!*—and, not feeling sure he was glad to be home, if this was home, he went home.

ELEVEN

"Well," said the stump mistress, as much to herself as to What-the-Dickens, "I can't imagine what young Pepper was thinking. She oughtn't to have led you here. Bad move on her part. You do seem too dull to be a spy—or if you are, the clan you're spying for is sorely lacking in the smarts department. They probably couldn't follow directions well enough to mount an attack on us anyway."

"I wouldn't attack anyone," said the orphan skibberee. "Why should I want to do that?"

"Oh, we're a clannish sort of creature; it's our lot in life," said Old Flossie. "We look after our own, which means in part overlooking everyone else."

"I don't have anyone who qualifies as 'my own,'" said What-the-Dickens, "and as far as 'everyone else' goes, that's Pepper and you and all those others I just saw. I'd hardly want to overlook you when I just met you. I wouldn't even know how."

"Live and learn," said Old Flossie. "Here we are." They had been descending steps all the while, but now she paused on a landing and took a great iron key out of her apron pocket. "I'll leave you to wash up in peace, and you'll find a little bedroom just beyond. It'll have to do."

"What will happen to Pepper?" he asked.

"That's her business, and none of yours," said Old Flossie, snappily. "Enjoy." She pushed him over the threshold, and he heard the door locking behind him.

Funny sort of welcome, he thought. *But there's so much for me to learn.*

A dim light filtered from above; he couldn't quite tell the source. The chamber was small and bare of even the simplest stool or cushion, and he couldn't find the bedroom she had promised. The walls were hung with a dense matting of vines sporting evil-looking thorny leaves.

She must have other things on her mind, he thought. *The stump mistress has forgotten that there's no sleeping chamber adjacent to this cell. She must be very busy with a job as a stump mistress. It sounds like a harder job than being a pet.*

Tired but not despondent, he sat cross-legged on the floor and lowered his chin into his hands. He thought about Pepper and hoped that she wouldn't get in trouble for bringing him here. Trouble was the last thing he had ever meant to make. Make good, maybe; make believe, yes. He wanted to make himself believe in something. But make trouble? Never.

Suddenly a hot storm of light flooded the chamber from above. The whole ceiling was burning white, too bright to look at. Invisible cords pulled the drapes of ivy back. On all the walls behind the ivy—even paneling the door through which he'd come—the silvery glint of mirror screamed at him. Showed him the truth: not one lost twin, as he'd once believed, but several images of sad, sorry What-the-Dickens, with his raked-up hair and his pretty wings with their useless, diamonding lights.

"Who are you?" brayed a voice from somewhere.

"What-the-Dickens, if you please," he answered.

"Who are you!" the voice repeated.

"What-the-Dickens!" he answered back, roaring a little, in case the invisible questioner was hard of hearing. Then he answered the same question five more times in a row, even though the voice got louder and louder, as if it could scare a different answer out of him.

But there was no other answer, not that he knew of.

"What is your colony?" the interviewer bellowed.

"I have no colony, I have no colony, I have no colony," he answered, to save the loud inquisitor a little time and breath.

"Where are you from?"

"Beyond, somewhere. It hasn't got a name, far as I know."

"Who are your friends?"

This one was harder. "A grisset and her young. A proud white cat named McCavity. A Bengal tiger called Maharajah. That's about it." He didn't think he could count as a friend the foul old woman who had trapped him in a drinking glass.

"What are you doing here?"

This was the hardest question of all. "I followed Pepper because she said, 'Let's go home.' I was trying to see if this was home." For the first time he began to lose his nerve a little. "Maybe I was wrong. Do you have to be so loud?"

"What are you doing here?"

"Hoping to get a little rest and then meet Doctor Ill, I guess? And make a home for myself with my own kind?"

"What are you doing here?"

The more often he heard this question, the less he was sure of the right answer. "Breathing? Waiting? Being scared? Watching myself in the mirror?"

"What are you doing here?"

"I don't know," he admitted. "I don't know."

"What are you doing here?"

He gave up. "What are *you* doing here?" he asked.

Suddenly the harsh light paled, and the vines rolled back into place on three walls. The fourth wall slid aside, revealing Old Flossie. She stood with her arms around her bosom, frowning a little.

"Since I've never known the question chamber to fail," she said, "I do believe you're not a spy. You're telling the truth."

"Was that you shouting all those questions at me?"

"Sorry about that. We have to take precautions. My voice is magnified through this seashell apparatus built into the wall."

"Wow. Cool. And all that light?"

"Heavy-duty torch that some human worker on the power lines left behind by accident. I say, you're curious enough to be a spy.

But I have to give you credit. I was watching from behind a two-way mirror. Pretty impressive, What-the-Whatever. You weren't even terrified of your own image. Usually it makes skibbereen crumple on the floor. Breaks their spirits, you see, softens them up for the interview."

"I didn't know that skibbereen are never seen until a little while ago," he explained. "So I haven't had time to become shy about it yet."

Old Flossie beckoned him closer, and stood aside. Behind her was a little bed snugly tucked into the wall. "I guess you've earned your rest. I'll go give an initial report to Doctor Ill, and when you're more yourself we can make the formal introductions. Somewhat to my surprise, you passed the test pretty well, young fellow. Especially for someone who seems so dim. But here's your bunk. There's a basin to the side; kindly splash yourself free of that tuna perfume. I'll let myself out."

He didn't believe he had fallen asleep— wasn't he too nervous to sleep?—but now Old Flossie was shaking him by the shoulder, saying, "Come on, dunderhead, it's almost dusk. Time to get up. I'll be back in five minutes with some dandelion wine."

She settled a firefly on a little wall sconce, where it could light the chamber, and she took herself off again, muttering.

What-the-Dickens blinked himself awake. He looked around. He had been so worn out that he hadn't noticed a thing about the little antechamber in which he'd been installed. The space was pleasant enough, a plain cell carved out—or perhaps eaten out—of the dry dead wood of the tree trunk. The walls were smoothed with rubbing and varnished nicely with some natural gloss, so they shone in the firefly-light.

He sat up. The mattress on which he'd fallen asleep was made of dried moss. He pushed aside a small silvery afghan crocheted out of strands of recycled spider's web. The pillow was several fluffy white dandelion heads stitched together—soft and agreeable, though he had to pick feathery bits out of his hair. What a cozy nest. He hoped he could sleep in this berth every day.

He stretched and flexed his wings and did some knee bends to loosen up. Then he arranged his trailing skin shreds to fall more neatly, as a tunic or a cape might. He was ready enough—as ready as he could get—when Old Flossie returned.

She twisted her lips, assessing his attempt at comeliness. Perhaps she was trying to smile and wasn't very good at it. "You're not much to look at; I'll give you that," she said, "but then that's the whole point with a skibberee, isn't it?"

She handed him a plastic screw-off cap from a discarded water bottle. It sloshed with a drink the color of antifreeze. "Here, help yourself to this decoction, duckie. Wet your whistle. I've brought you a bite of crystallized honey, too. I let you sleep as long as I could, but the compound is gathering for our Duty Day revelry. If you're really an orphan as you claim to be, much of the goings-on will be new to you. You'll learn something about Undertree Common, I reckon."

"Undertree Common?"

"The homey name for it. Technically we're Northwest Sector, Division B. Come along."

He came along.

They left the guest bedchamber and followed some steps down. He guessed they were dropping deeper into the trunk of the tree, perhaps down its central taproot. When the staircase was met by other descending flights, the steps widened and the treads became deeper—much the way an accumulation of rivulets will broaden into a stream.

There must be dozens, maybe hundreds of rooms beneath the old tree stump, each with its own private entrance. Each with its own potential friend, thought What-the-Dickens, stirred by happy anxiety. And one of them was Pepper's room. Where was she?

Then the flight of steps turned a corner and finished through an elegant carved archway. What-the-Dickens and the stump mistress came out upon a gallery looking down into a wide and plunging underground coliseum.

The cave had been laboriously carved out under the old tree. What-the-Dickens could see tree roots high overhead in the packed earth, trained like grapevines to form a dome. The ribs of the roots were tied back in places, and embellished here and there with carvings of florets or the faces of ancestors. It wasn't so much an auditorium, exactly, as a kind of town square.

Several hundred skibbereen murmured excitedly. They were all on foot, pushing to get what seats there were, or jostling for prime places on the floor. They were getting ready to watch something on the stage in front.

"Why don't they fly up and perch along the walls?" asked What-the-Dickens.

"We frown on flying indoors, because even in the best of circumstances it isn't easy for skibbereen to control their wings," said Old Flossie. "You'll have noticed that yourself, simpleton though you seem to be. The tight quarters of this compound have led to many accidentally slapped faces, impromptu duels, grievances and griefs and untimely deaths. It is simply safer to walk."

"Oh," said What-the-Dickens. He was sorry he had asked, for skibbereen were turning at the sound of Old Flossie's lecture. He felt the eyes of the collective upon him.

He didn't sense overt hostility, nor did he imagine warmth or real welcome.

He supposed it was caution, and he supposed that was a good thing. There were other colonies, he had deduced, and so it was reasonable for the skibbereen to imagine he might be an enemy, even if he wasn't.

Shall I wave, to show them I'm friendly? he thought, but decided against it. He was too shy, and anyway, waving might look dorky.

He was glad when Old Flossie led him forward to a narrow carved bench in a section up front marked "Reserved." Pepper was waiting for him there. She was nibbling the edge of her wing tip.

"Hi, Pepper!" he said, perhaps too exuberantly, for all the skibbereen in the nearby rows fell about laughing and echoing, "Hi, Pepper! Hi, Pepper! Hi, Pepper!"

"Oh, do shut up," said Pepper, and they did, but their smirks didn't stop smirking. More quietly, she commented, "I am glad to see you. I was afraid they'd concluded you were an enemy alien and—"

"And what?"

"—Well . . . it would have been my fault if they'd—"

"If they'd what?"

"Never mind," she said breezily, straightening up. "No harm done. Happy endings, and all that."

"Did you get your credits?" asked What-the-Dickens, grabbing her hand as he sat down.

"Don't touch me. Skibbereen rarely touch each other."

All these rules, he thought. *I'll never learn.*

"Please," she said. "Don't be glum. I'm glad you're okay. Now, shhh: The pageant's about to start. Look, there's Doctor Ill."

Old Flossie settled down on the other

side of What-the-Dickens and dragged some handiwork out of a sack. She armed herself with two thorns shaped into knitting needles. A wodge of curlicued metallic scrubbing pad supplied the thread. "I knit handcuffs as a hobby," explained Old Flossie happily, and set to work. "Idle hands get up to no good, so I like to be prepared in case I meet up with any idle hands."

What-the-Dickens glanced to where Pepper was pointing. Above the stage area, in a kind of private theater box for Very Important Personalities, a husky skibberee had appeared. Oh, the stateliness of a statesman. Broad of belly but narrow of chin, goateed and pomaded and laced into a tartan vest, Doctor Ill waved with a grand plump hand at the crowd below. The loyal skibbereen roared their greeting back. It took What-the-Dickens a moment to realize that Doctor Ill was sitting on the back of a muzzled mouse.

"He's been crippled for quite a while," whispered Pepper. "Some time back, he lost the use of his legs in a horrible dental accident."

"The poor mouse," said What-the-Dickens. "Does it like its muzzle?"

"Who knows?" Pepper shrugged. "It's all muzzled up so it can't talk."

What-the-Dickens began to reply, but Pepper added, "That's *just* a joke. Mice can't talk, you little fruit fly."

"Oh," he said.

"Let the Duty Pageant begin!" called Doctor Ill, waving a cane made out of a porcupine quill. The hubbub below simmered down, and the fireflies in the ceiling of the coliseum dimmed their lights to quarter-strength.

❧ TWELVE ❧

A small but sprightly orchestra offstage somewhere struck up a merry tune, and the curtains were pulled back.

"Ohhhhhhhhhh!" gasped everyone.

"It's the same every time," whispered Pepper. "I don't know why they always act so surprised." Old Flossie leaned in front of What-the-Dickens and rapped Pepper's knees with a knitting needle to make her hush.

The overture crashed to a close in a rapture of cymbals. A chorus of bees bumbled onstage and took its place on a kind of bleachers made out of old Popsicle sticks. The bees hummed in less-than-perfect thirds.

Next, in strict formation, some male skibbereen marched on with red plastic toothbrushes slung over their shoulders like military firearms. They came to a halt on either side of a podium made of two old wooden spools, now bare of thread. One spool stood atop the other, secured together by a nail driven through their centers.

The music of the bees droned toward a climax. Finally a glorious female skibberee, in a skirt made out of a Sunday newspaper color supplement, paraded onstage. Rapturous applause from all sides. "Why does her dress say 'Parade'?" asked What-the-Dickens.

"Shhh," said everyone.

"Greetings, Doctor Ill," began the silky-voiced hostess. "Greetings to all the loyal residents of Northwest Sector, Division B: our own Undertree Common! My name is Silviana, and I love you with all my heart!" She blew kisses at one and all.

"I love you back!" cried What-the-Dickens, smitten. But when all the skibbereen took up his cry, it wasn't entirely in mockery, and Silviana pouted and preened and cut capers till the applause died down.

"You don't talk back to a star!" hissed Pepper. "Just shut up and listen."

"Oh, sorry," whispered What-the-Dickens.

Silviana went on. The rustling of newsprint followed her as she drifted from side to side of the stage, displaying to each and every skibberee in the room her personal glamour.

"Every month at the full moon," sang out Silviana, "we gather to remember our humble origins as skibbereen. We recall our ancestors. We relish our relatives. We refresh our sense of mission. Also we refrain from putting old chewing gum on the undersides of the benches. This means you. Let the Pageant begin!"

"Bravo!" shouted Doctor Ill, so swept away that he slipped sideways on his muzzled mouse. Silviana tossed him a sunburst of a smile as she took her place at the podium.

"Remember, if you will, the dark days of the past," sang Silviana, as the bees transposed their melody into a minor mode. "Long ago, when the First Fairy accidentally arrived, she was as mysterious and clueless and unmotivated as a common butterfly in some common meadow!"

At this, a few skibbereen came drifting in from offstage. Some were dressed as mouse-brown moths, some as monarch butterflies, orange as Maharajah. Thanks to the skill of a cunning costumier, one of them sported wings cut out of an old dial of plastic laminates originally intended to color the light cast upon an aluminum Christmas tree. Her costume wings were flashy, outsized, and ridiculous. But the magical effect was a winner. "Ooooh!" said everyone, several times in a row.

What-the-Dickens began to applaud the spectacle. He couldn't help himself. *This is the best part of my life so far,* he thought.

Silviana started to narrate the natural history of the skibbereen, in a fluting voice that carried clear to the back of the chamber.

"More than a century ago, a poor old lepidopterist—meaning a butterfly scientist, people; pay attention now—lived in the woods with his poor wife, whose name was Edith. One day the husband caught sight of what he thought was an unknown specimen clinging to a cabbage. He declared it a 'true fritillary.' *Fritillary* is the name of a certain sort of spotted butterfly."

Out from the wings came a skibberee acting the part of the butterfly expert. He wore a caped jacket and a sort of deerstalker hat, very Sherlock Holmes, fashioned out of an upside-down acorn shell. With a great deal of effort, he managed to balance before him a genuine magnifying glass—the real item—sized for human use.

This made his face look huge.

When the scientist looked directly at them through his lens, What-the-Dickens screamed along with the rest of the audience. It was like being spotted by a predator. *Skibbereen are never seen!* He began to understand the panic of being noticed.

It was kind of fun, and terrible, too, both at once.

The butterfly expert turned away and pretended instead to search for butterflies. Most of them fled in terror, but a single one trembled delicately in place, allowing the inspection to proceed. This was the gaudy one with carnival wings.

Then out came the scientist's wife, Edith, played by a skibberee lass in an apron cut from a white paper napkin. Somehow, on her tender shoulders she balanced the better part of a plastic face torn from an abandoned toy baby doll. The head was about eight sizes too large for the body that barely managed to hold it upright. The effect was decidedly monstrous. But this, perhaps, is how humans appear to skibbereen.

The eyes of the doll-wife stared glassily ahead as if listening to the narration.

Silviana continued. "The scientist had a problem with his overbite. His diction was lousy. His tongue curled and spittle lashed everywhere. Did his wife, Edith, hear him say 'true fritillary'?"

"No," the audience clamored.

"Did she hear 'tooth fertility'?"

"No."

"Did she hear 'true virility'?"

"No!" shrieked the audience. They seemed familiar with this exchange, and were eager to respond.

"What," said Silviana stagily, "did she *think* he said?"

The audience roared. "Tooth fairy! Tooth fairy!"

"I have no doubt!" agreed Silviana, and continued. "Over tea that afternoon the wife took up her pen, and she scribbled a story."

Edith Monster-Babyface now swept up from the floor a jay's feather, brilliantly blue and black, and she mimed dipping it in an imaginary bottle of ink and writing words across the floor. "The wife called her story 'Tooth Fairy Magic.' It was all about how a sweet little tooth fairy collects baby teeth and pays for them in cold hard cash, something of which the family was in short supply."

"Imagine!" the skibbereen said with a laugh. "A tooth fairy! Ha-ha!"

"The wife read her story aloud to her lepidopterist husband. He said, 'Edith, you'll turn our children mushy in the head with such nonsense!' The children, however, clapped with glee."

From the opposite wing, extras playing the couple's children plowed onto the stage and sat down around Edith Monster-Babyface. They swayed back and forth in time as if in thrall to her rapturous tale.

The butterfly thing that was neither a true fritillary nor a tooth fairy struck a pose in the middle of the stage. Eventually stagehands, remembering their cue, pushed out from the wings a box of kitchen matches standing on its end. It had been painted over with a clock-face, though the numbers were all helter-skelter. (1:00 a.m., 2:00 p.m., 6:45, 4:00 b.m., 9:15 ½, 8:70; 7:00 p.m.; 90.9 FM; 26:10, and back around to 1:00 a.m.)

"And when Edith read her story," said Silviana, "the lone skibberee, the First Fairy, the foundress of our species, listened to it. From whatever realm of faerie she had accidentally blundered, she had to make herself up anew in this new world. So she listened hard. And she began to evolve, because stories work their magic that way. They build conviction and erode conviction in equal measure."

The gaudily winged creature went and stood behind the clock, as if listening, while Edith Monster-Babyface mimed reading her tooth fairy story with many broad and sentimental effects.

"In time," continued Silviana, "Edith sold the story to a children's magazine called *Saint Nicholas*. Thomas Nast, who first drew Santa Claus to look the way he does today, illustrated the piece. He pictured the Tooth Fairy as a simpery airborne dance-hall girl, conducting a campaign of dental hygiene with her sidekick, an androgynous flying toothbrush named Tickles."

Here Silviana herself cut a few figures, looking inane and attractive. She danced in tandem with a skibberee who had a toothbrush tied on his back. The bristly head of it, painted with a pair of goo-goo eyes, towered above her. The audience nearly wet itself with delight.

"Slowly, the notion of a tooth fairy took hold. Tickles the flying toothbrush, however, proved less popular, and he was quickly re-tired." The toothbrush walked offstage in a huff, and Silviana returned to her podium.

"In human legend, the Tooth Fairy pos-sesses a very low-grade magic. But its inspi-ration—our ancestress—the creature consid-ered by the scientist to be a new specimen of spotted butterfly—was, magically speaking, rather talented, too."

Skibbereen the room over were with-drawing handkerchiefs from their pockets and blowing their noses. This was the good part.

"You see, the figure skulking behind the clock had been known in the hidden other world as a skibberee. Through no fault of her own, this nameless skibberee, the First Fairy, the mother of us all, happened to mutate, in that lighthearted, civilization-threatening way that species do. The mutation caused her to lose her protective coloring—her invisibili-ty—and to be lodged, without hope of re-turn, in the tide of human affairs, otherwise known as Our World."

Silviana flung her arms out wide to em-phasize Our World.

"The world at large; and it *is* large."

Huge applause for the world at large.

"Newly shipwrecked in our dangerous

world, the mutated skibberee had few instincts on which to draw. She was scared, naïve, and suggestible. When she heard the story of the Tooth Fairy, she believed it was all about her."

The butterfly-skibberee behind the clock stepped out into the spotlight and clapped her hands to suggest sudden revelation.

"The lone skibberee paid as much attention as her raw nervous system could manage. Having arrived from the Magical Beyond while in a state of pregnancy, she produced an egg sac. In just a few generations, what remained of her original skibberee proclivities had been reshaped by the species' self-determination as Tooth Fairies.

"And so, ladies and gentlefriends, was our kind established. Our job was spelled out for us. Our civilization chose to fulfill its mission: to work hard and to thrive. Aided by our natural love of secrecy, magic, and good cheer, we skibbereen have found ourselves a duty and pledged ourselves to our task.

"Please rise and join in singing the Tooth Fairy Anthem."

What-the-Dickens, amazed at the power of great theater, was swept to his feet. Though he didn't know the words, he listened with tears in his eyes as his kin and kith, his own beloved kind, bellowed their national carol. The audience sang along with Silviana, Edith Monster-Babyface, the Honor Guard, the butterflies, the children, the lepidopterist, Tickles the Toothbrush, and the actress playing the First Fairy.

> *Mine eyes have seen the glory*
> *of a wobbling baby tooth.*
> *If you poke it with your tongue enough,*
> *you just might knock it looth.*
> *It's an awfully gory story,*
> *but I'm telling you the truth:*
> *That tooth is coming out!*
> *Leave it somewhere we can get it,*
> *You will find you don't regret it.*
> *We will pay you, cash or credit:*
> *That tooth is coming out!*

The room erupted in cheers. Pink balloons, fashioned from prechewed bubble gum, were released from the ceiling. Ticker tape—made from the raveled edges of newspapers—fell everywhere. Silviana took a half a dozen bows. From his private box, Doctor Ill himself tossed the star a bouquet of violets wrapped up in party ribbons. "It's the best thing I ever saw," wept What-the-Dickens in joy.

"Get used to it," said Pepper, who wasn't clapping. "It doesn't change at all, month by month, year in, year out. It's our history, for good or for ill."

"Is it true?"

Pepper shrugged. "It's true that this is what we tell ourselves. Is the history accurate? Who knows? How could we know one way or the other? Does it matter? It's a pretty enough story."

The crowd was chanting, *Free the tooth! Free the tooth!*

"Can I meet Silviana?"

"In your dreams," barked Old Flossie, wiping her eyes on her sleeve. "She doesn't condescend to notice the likes of you, laddio. Besides, you have an appointment with Doctor Ill. Pepper is to take you to his den at once."

She blew her nose loudly. "I do love to be reminded of our duty," she said, and cuffed Pepper on the shoulder. "And so should you, Pepper. Now get going, you, and don't keep the good Doctor waiting."

❦ ❦ ❦

"Are you asleep?" whispered Gage.

"I don't know. Maybe I was," said Dinah, sitting up. "Were you?"

"I thought I was telling you about the Duty Pageant, but perhaps I was just thinking about it. My eyes were closed."

"I thought I was listening about it," she replied, "but maybe I was kind of dreaming about it."

She shook her head. Everything was clumping together in her mind and getting mixed up. Brittney and Juliette out in the fitful world, and the raging winds at work, and the flying of skibbereen through the night: it made her confused.

She tried harder to organize what she could be sure of. That was her best talent, after all.

✦ Rebecca Ruth and Zeke are here asleep.

That was about it.

"Look: Zeke and Rebecca Ruth are both out like lights," she murmured, pointing to them.

Rebecca Ruth lay hunched, her little behind slightly elevated under her knees, her face turned to one side. In her sleep she clutched her stuffed lamb in a stranglehold.

Zeke, beyond, was entirely lost in a mess of blankets, sleeping so still that they couldn't even hear his breathing.

"Well, if I was asleep, I'm not asleep anymore," said Dinah. "Is the wind dying down? Maybe the quiet woke me up. You might as well tell me what happened to Pepper. I like her. Why is she called that, anyway?"

❧ THIRTEEN ❧

"Why are you called Pepper?" said What-the-Dickens, as they walked back up staircases into the tree trunk.

"You do ask a lot of questions," she commented.

"Pepper," he said. "Why Pepper?"

"I'm trying to tell you. Don't be a thistle-head. To understand where the names come from, you gotta understand our culture. That little pantomime—who knows if any of it is true? But here we skibbereen are, side by side with a bigger, treacherous world. We keep to ourselves as much as we can. We don't steal and we don't borrow: we pay for what we take."

"I'll pay you if you tell me why you're called Pepper." He was teasing her. This was teasing. It made him feel gingery inside. Or maybe peppery.

How amazing to feel calm enough to feel peppery or gingery. *Is this what it means to feel at home?* he wondered.

Pepper snapped, "Stop grinning like a hoptoad with a big old fly rolled up in his tongue. I'm telling you. Now listen: Every colony of skibbereen gets its own system of naming. We borrow our names from the first set of words we see—but we change them. Undertree Common was founded, let's see, two plus one plus one plus two more years ago. More or less. Give or take. That's when the highway was going in, see, and this bit of woods was cut off from human foot traffic."

"Why here?"

"Rural skibbereen often use highway cloverleafs for their settlements. Out of the way, conveniently cut off, yet centrally located—all at once. While barreling by at forty miles an hour, what human nudnik could spot the odd skibberee? In cities, I'm told, it's a different story—colonies in water towers at the top of skyscrapers, in abandoned subway tunnels, etc. But I'll never know much about that. However good I do, that'll be way beyond me."

"What are you, a historian? I'm asking about your name. Your name. Pepper, Pepper, Pepper."

"Shut up. I'm telling you, okay? At the time that the settlers discovered this available tree trunk, they also saw in the underbrush a few discarded pages of newspaper advertising. Hawking the wares of some local pharmacy. So our colony harvests its names from the words we find in that bit of text. So our names are things like Intyfresh, Clea, Spirin, Olga, Flossie, Doctor Ill, Outhwash. But they derive from human words like *mintyfresh, clean, aspirin, Colgate, floss, pill,* and *mouthwash.* Me, I'm Pepper, derived from *peppermint.*"

He liked it. He liked her. "What about Silviana?"

"She broke the rule and named herself."

Sort of like me, thought What-the-Dickens, but didn't say so. "Are there many skibbereen in the world?"

"Whether humans know it or not, the truth is there are lots more than one Tooth Fairy. Dozens of tooth fairies work in any given sector during any given season of tooth decay. Most of them are nameless, harmless skibbereen stationed at their division headquarters. They do their jobs; they go home to sleep and dream of teeth; they get up; they brush and gargle; they go back to work."

"It sounds wonderful to have a real mission in life. A home, a family, a vocation."

"*Wonderful* might be the word some would use. But not everyone. Not me."

He raised his eyebrow.

"Oh, what would you know? You're a natural born idiot. Most of the skibbereen never get more than a few feet from their native colonies. *In their whole lives,* What-the-Dickens. The lowers are born together in a heap. In a heap they work like slaves together, and together in a heap they die. Only if you get to be an Agent of Change do you get out at all. The world is a honey of a place, full of intrigue and novelty. But skibbereen have to stay hidden if they want to stay alive. Being abroad without a license is a big no-no."

He didn't quite get the concept of being born *in a heap,* but he could hear the feeling in her voice. "So that's why you want your license so much."

"Now you're catching on." She lowered her voice. "Life here is just fine if you got no curiosity—and most of them don't. But some of us do, and getting licensed to do active duty is a must. I'd die of boredom otherwise."

"You've got a personal name—Pepper. Isn't that a sign of something?"

"It's provisional. I could easily lose my name and go back to being known by my job title."

"I want to be an Agent of Change too,"

said What-the-Dickens. "Will you teach me?"

"It's not up to me," said Pepper. "And anyway, ain't you listening? *We don't work in pairs.* Got it? If even one of us is ever accidentally seen by a human, we do our best to imitate a mutant wasp or a butterfly. Often we end up being sprayed with Raid or Flit or the like. We have to be free to live alone and die alone, to preserve the safety of the colony. We have to pretend we got no names, no lives, no futures. We have to be nobodies."

What-the-Dickens said, "Well, I come with a lot of practice feeling like a nobody. I'll fit right in." He grinned at her, but in truth he was feeling very like somebody just at present.

"Don't get too comfy here," she warned him. "We're not good with strangers. The truth is, we're a funny little race of critter. We're neither bird nor mammal. I doubt we have butterfly ancestors, but we're not an idiotic little fairy tale come to life, either. We don't know what we are. We only know what we do. That's about all we can count on."

"What did you mean when you said we were born in a heap?" Maybe he could learn something about his origins now.

They had reached a broad door that had

DOCTOR ILL painted on it in shiny silver letters. Pepper looked this way and that; the corridor was empty in both directions. "We mustn't be late," she said. "Everyone's super-punctual around here. Even a clock has teeth, we're told, and time has a bite all of its own. But if you shut up and stop asking so many questions, I'll rattle off everything I know about the subject. Which ain't a lot."

She sketched in the natural history of the skibbereen as best she could. In short order What-the-Dickens learned that his sort was usually hatched in dollops of seventy to ninety at a time.

As Pepper described it, the science seemed distinctly vague. But What-the-Dickens deduced that in her last few days of pregnancy, a mother skibberee, weighed down by her egg sac, doesn't usually get around much. Most often she settles in the notch of a tree limb. Then she gets to work. She gnaws through the filaments and netting of her sac to expose her eggs to light, so they can heat up enough to hatch.

By this point she is pretty exhausted. She's happy to let sunlight finish the good job she started. When she feels peckish she nibbles on the discarded filaments, which are crunchy, like strands of celery string: stuffed with nutrition, and tasty besides.

Usually she looks over her eggs—thirty-nine here and seventeen there and twenty-four over there, and a funny leftover one clumped on the stem—her lovely eggs! Like a froth of soap bubbles. She can never quite add them up—seventy-nine, eighty-one, or was it seventy-seven?—but does it matter? She loves them all.

Sooner or later her hatchlings start to emerge. A whole new population of skibbereen appears almost at once. When the air hits them, they grow at once. Within a minute the skibbereen newborns are as tall as they'll ever be: three inches, four max.

"But where did the rest of my hatchlings go?" asked What-the-Dickens. "Where did I come from?"

"Basically, no one ever knows the answer to *that* question," said Pepper. "I mean, think of the Duty Pageant: skibbereen as a species ain't got a clue where they came from. Your question is just a bit more personal than everyone else's. You'll get used to it. Don't worry."

She straightened her shoulders and wetted

her fingers and pressed down the seams of her wing tips, working out the wrinkles. "Now mind your manners and look smart—at least as smart as you can, given your looks," she whispered. "The doctor is a good old codger, but he's formal, and he can't stand an uppity skibberee. Gets on his nerves to be talked back to. And I can't afford to frost him."

What-the-Dickens squared his shoulders. *I've survived the solitary interview,* he thought. *This should be a piece of cake.* "Ready when you are."

Pepper knocked. A cutting, superior voice responded. "Enter, at once!" The word *enter* came out more like *Eye-YEN-ter!*

They came through as directed. The room was a single shaft of blond wood tapering upward to a point, like a conical tent. Suspended on strings from the ceiling hung a wooden object, lovingly lit by fireflies penned into recesses. "What is that?" said What-the-Dickens.

Doctor Ill looked up from his desk. "Who are . . . ?—Oh, yes." He consulted his notes. "A rogue tooth fairy, I'm told. How novel. How charming. You look perfectly ordinary, in a raffish, obliterated sort of way. But darling boy, you don't ask the questions here. I do."

"Oops. Sorry," said What-the-Dickens.

Doctor Ill leaned his elbows forward on the padded leather patches that covered the worn spots on the sleeves of his shirt. Nearby in its cage, his muzzled mouse quivered and looked either timid or mortified, or both.

"Settle down, dear," he said to it, with-drawing a fragment of shredded carrot from a stack of old small matchboxes piled one on top of another like a chest of drawers. "Here, Muzzlemutt, have a carrot. It's just a skibberee you haven't met yet."

Doctor Ill fed the carrot to the mouse, who could hardly eat it due to the muzzle, but gummed it ferociously into carrot juice.

"Poor pet," said What-the-Dickens. "Is he scared of me?"

"He's scared of skibbereen who ask ques-tions," said Doctor Ill.

Pepper kicked What-the-Dickens in the calf, but not before he had pointed question-ingly at the wooden object hanging over the Doctor's desk.

"You're amused by the premier piece in my art collection. You have taste, dear boy. What is your name?"

After a silence, Pepper muttered, "You can answer the Doctor now."

"What-the-Dickens," he said.

Doctor Ill picked up his cane from behind his desk and pointed at the sculpture. "That masterwork is said to be one of the original wooden teeth carved for the jaw of George Washington. Of course it could be a forgery, but it's still impressive, no? 'I cannot tell a lie: I have a false tooth!'" Doctor Ill laughed at his own joke, but no one else got it.

"It's called the crown jewel," whispered Pepper to What-the-Dickens, with a little bob in the direction of Doctor Ill. "And he who rules underneath it is the crown. That's Doctor Ill."

"Wow." What-the-Dickens was amazed. "Where'd it come from?"

"Enough about that." Doctor Ill turned to Pepper. "I don't know where you picked up this vague fellow, but I suggest you bring him back where you got him. I've been advised he's not a spy, and that is good. Still, he's clearly not our sort at all."

"I'm not?" said What-the-Dickens.

Doctor Ill looked displeased at the sound of a question.

"Please forgive him, sir," said Pepper, attempting a curtsy, though it looked more as if she was delivering herself of a pressure of gas. "He don't know any better. He's an orphan, he tells me, who has never met another of his kind before yesterday. I've been trying to read him the riot act and all but he's a bit, well, slow. He can't put two and two together to come up with, well, whatever it is."

"Interesting," said Doctor Ill, "but not my concern. We take care of our own, Pepper, and we don't fraternize with rabble."

"What was I to do, sir? He just showed up—"

"No questions!" Doctor Ill was harsh with Pepper, perhaps because she ought to know better. "Now listen, Pepper. You had a job to fulfill. You arrived back at base a few minutes after sunrise. We don't muck about here with excuses. You have violated your probationary period and failed to satisfy the committee. I will give you liberty to deliver this alien back to the wild, but when you return you must surrender your name and your hopes of a license. No Agent of Change appointment for you. You will learn to be happy in a menial task. That is your lot: you have shown us so yourself by your failure to follow the rules."

Pepper hung her head.

"It was all my fault!" cried What-the-Dickens. "Don't blame her, sir! She couldn't help it that I discovered her and interrupted her in her mission. Don't penalize her. Penalize me instead, why don't you?"

Doctor Ill sighed and put his hand to his chest. "No one knows the private costs of being a public servant." He fortified himself with a sip of something that smelled nutty-sweet. "You can't be expected to understand, dear lad, the ways of our colony. Be grateful you weren't slaughtered by skittish skibbereen manning the stump runway."

"I am grateful, and I wasn't slaughtered because Pepper was with me," said What-the-Dickens. He was urgent and earnest both. "Please, sir. Good doctor. It isn't right to punish her just because she was nice to a lost skibberee."

The Doctor took another sip and studied the airborne tooth as if looking for guidance in its crevasses.

Finally he sighed, and shook his head as he spoke. "I am a kind soul. Kindness has always been my curse. So I will grant you one more chance, Pepper. I'll give you an assignment to-night. But it will be harder than usual, because you must make up for your tardiness on the recent mission. You must prove yourself worthy."

"You are *totally* kind," said Pepper.

"Your assignment will come in over the network in the usual manner," said Doctor Ill. He picked up the porcupine cane again and pointed it at Pepper. It looked like a long, treacherous stinger. "But you must take this interloper with you and lose him somewhere. That's the price you pay for your extra chance. You must return to base with your next assigned tooth—alone."

"Oh, now listen—" began Pepper, but she fell silent at the stern look of the Doctor.

"We cannot integrate with the likes of him," said the Doctor. "He is a foreign element. As such, he is more risky to us than you know. Sweet fool that he is, he can have little idea about how skibbereen colonies work. If he is an orphan, I regret it. But he is not one of us and he may not become one of us. I say this with passion and sorrow, for I am a tolerant creature, myself. (Everyone says so, and they're right.) Still, that is my decision. Do you understand?"

"Do I have a choice?" replied Pepper in a small voice.

The Doctor didn't answer. What-the-Dickens said, with as little bite in his tone as he could manage, "Well? Does she?"

"You know what happens if we make allowances," said Doctor Ill. "No, of course you don't, for you are innocent and stupid. Have you ever heard of decay?"

What-the-Dickens had not ever heard of decay.

"It threatens us," said Doctor Ill in a short voice. "And if we should let up our guard, dear boy, all would be lost. We can't and we don't make allowances for . . . peculiarity. All stoutness of effect is lost if one starts accounting for peculiarity. Decay is softness, you see; permissiveness, cloudiness of thought, and sentimentality."

All would be lost for you, maybe, thought What-the-Dickens. *But I started out lost. I have just been found. I've just witnessed my first-ever Duty Pageant. I'm reporting for duty. That's not softness. That's strict obedience.*

"I think," said What-the-Dickens, "I deserve a chance to prove myself not especially peculiar. Isn't that fair?"

"Oh, fair," said Doctor Ill. "Well, if you're

going to talk about fair . . ." He looked at What-the-Dickens a little more closely. "Perhaps setting you your own task *would* be the appropriate thing to do. But I can't afford to be fair to everyone. I'm done with this chatter. Accept the task, Pepper, and accept the price of my judgment, you What-the-Nutcase person. Accept it, or decline it and go about your business, in which case you would be stripped of your name at once and denied your license to fly abroad. As for What-the-Dickens — well, if you stick around here when I've told you to go, I can't answer for what happens to you. You are dismissed."

"Thank you, *sir*," said Pepper in a hushed and startled voice. "I suppose we accept. We have no other choice, really."

"Before we leave," said What-the-Dickens, "may I ask one other thing? Even though I'm not supposed to ask anything?"

Doctor Ill didn't deny the petition. He just closed his eyes and waited.

"What does skibbereen mean, even?"

The Doctor recited from memory. "*Skibberee,* singular; *skibbereen,* plural. From the verb intransitive, *skibberow* [Middle English *skippen* from Old Norse *skeappa*]: to skip about *(archaic).*"

"Thank you for that, anyway," said What-the-Dickens.

They backed out. As they closed the door behind them so softly it hardly made a click, the mouse mewed in relief or regret; they couldn't tell.

Pepper gripped his hand. "Thank you," she said to him.

"Skibbereen don't touch each other," he reminded her, but grinningly. "Did I do okay?"

"You did swell. You did terrific. We'll work out something. Your life is reprieved, and I have an extension of my license application: one more mission, one more chance. Let's hurry up and launch. We'll invent the rest as we go along."

"Where are we hurrying to?" asked What-the-Dickens.

"First stop, the bank vault," said Pepper. "We have to stock up with some change."

"Change? Because you're an Agent of Change?"

But Pepper was too excited to answer his questions. She hurried ahead, on tiptoes made swifter by the lift of an illegal wing swipe from time to time. He followed her deeper into the bowels of Undertree Common, toward the central bank. They hadn't gone far when he —

⊰⊱ ⊰⊱ ⊰⊱

"What's that?" said Gage.

"What?" said Dinah.

"Get down!" said Gage. He threw out his arm and hit her on the shoulder. She slumped to the floor.

A flashlight shone through the window, and the doorknob rattled, and rattled again, harder. The noise of footsteps going around the corner of the house. The sound of something pausing.

Dinah was now sure that the wind had died down sometime during the night, when they were deep in the story of the orphan skibberee. It must have. She could hear so clearly, too clearly, the slick of feet on wet grass, and then the crunch of feet on gravel, and then the sound of the side door being tried. It was locked, but less securely so, and from the outside, someone put his weight against it and began to shove against it to break in.

One time, twice, another time.

Not to be scared. Don't be scared. It could be

   ✦

   ✦

or even

   ✦

But Dinah couldn't imagine any help convincing enough to vanquish the terrors—in her mind and in the breezeway.

The sound of splitting wood. The sound of rain dripping off the eaves of the garage, suddenly louder once the lock gave way and the door opened.

THE WITCHING HOUR

"I—" SAID DINAH IN A WHISPER, but Gage clapped his hand over her mouth. He put his finger to his lips and pulled the blanket up to her chin. *Pretend you're asleep. At once!*

But she couldn't keep her eyes closed.

She tried again to organize the new fears storming her. She did a better job this time, though she wasn't all that happy to come up with

+ a bear from the hills
+ a mountain cat, though could cats do doorknobs?
+ a juvenile delinquent
+ a tramp needing shelter
+ a scavenger
+ worse.

She got stuck at the "worse" notions. Then she couldn't think her thoughts backward to the less scary ones, even though she tried.

Maybe her mother was right. Imagination *was* a dangerous talent. The disasters she could imagine all too well . . .

Gage was on his knees looking for something to use in defense. The closest thing to hand was an ornamental poker near the fireplace. He grasped this and whisked it in the air once or twice to judge its heft. Dinah could see the look of self-disgust on his face. As if he couldn't believe what he seemed about to do.

And Dinah could hardly believe it either. He looked ridiculous. Decent, long-winded Gage! But he was getting ready. Ready for whatever.

She saw a scissoring of torchlights in the breezeway and she picked up a muttering of voices. Whoever was here was making an effort to be secret. So they must guess that the house was occupied — even though it was dark, even though the neighborhood had largely been evacuated. What had tipped them off?

And what could they want? There was no food to speak of. Looters wouldn't look kindly on two jars of mashed carrots prepared for discriminating diners aged twelve to eighteen months.

Gage went from a kneeling position to a crouch.

Dinah waved furiously at him to get his attention. Could he read her lips in the gloom? With two fingers, she mimed racing away. She didn't need to whisper the words: *Should we run out the front door? The wind's died down. . . .*

He only frowned and swept his hand toward where Rebecca Ruth and Zeke were lost in their blankets, dead asleep. He was right. They wouldn't be able to rouse Zeke fast enough. And Rebecca Ruth would cry like the dickens.

What is *the dickens,* Dinah found herself wondering, somewhat excitedly, as if the answer to that question was the answer to everything.

She got up on her haunches, despite her cousin's instructions. The only thing she could reach was Rebecca Ruth's stuffed lamb, Tiger. Dinah grabbed it anyway and held it. If she had to, she would fling it in the face of the first intruder.

Dinah knew this action—tossing a stuffed lamb in the face of an invader—would be against the Ormsby family creed of charity to all. But it might buy them an eighth of a second. It was worth the risk.

"We're going to have to wake them," said a man's voice, "since they haven't heard us yet."

"Well, talk to them from here, then," came a woman's voice, scratchy with fatigue, "or you'll freak them into an early grave."

"I'll do it," said a third voice—a familiar, testy voice. The hunched silhouette of Zeke showed up in the doorway.

"You!" said Gage.

Dinah looked over, and then kicked the heap of blankets that she had thought was Zeke. No Zeke.

"You're awake," said Zeke, sounding both relieved and guilty.

"What's going on?" Gage's voice was lower than natural. "Where have you been? Who's there with you?" His voice got louder, a little throttled. Rebecca Ruth didn't even stir, so Dinah checked again to make sure her sister was still there, too. She was.

"Deputy, county sheriff's office," said the man's voice. "Name of Campbell. Frank Campbell. Sorry if we alarmed you. We did try to open your door from the outside but, uh, seems it had locked behind this young fellow when he left earlier."

Deputy Campbell trudged in, a slope-shouldered older man in a windbreaker zigzagged with reflective tape. His brushy ivory-white moustache dripped with rain. An associate followed, a thickset, pint-size Hispanic woman in a yellow slicker. They both lugged industrial-strength flashlights that looked uncomfortably heavy.

"Um, my colleague, Rosa Herrera," said Deputy Campbell. He sounded uncomfortable with the formality. Normally at this hour he probably was at home asleep with his TV on mute, thought Dinah. "We're dispatched from the county sheriff's office, like I said. On citizen patrol. This your boy, I guess? We found him across the road, finishing up a break-and-enter. You can drop the poker, by the way."

"Ezekiel Ormsby," said Gage. "What in the blazes do you think you're doing? And when did you leave? And where did you go?" Gage was on his feet by now. He didn't put the poker down entirely, but held it at his side like a rolled umbrella.

"Answer the question, sir," Deputy Campbell said heavily to Gage. "Your kids?"

"He's under my care, as ought to be obvious," said Gage.

"You're not the boss of me," Zeke said to Gage.

"Not your son?" asked Deputy Campbell.

"No. A cousin," answered Gage.

"Look, cuz," interrupted Deputy Herrera, "this district was cleared out several days ago. You're not supposed to be here. This patrol is going to cost the taxpayers a bundle. Sorry to be blunt, but we're going to have to move you out to the emergency relief station. Over to Swanson's Gymnastics on the valley road, because we can't get down the other way, not with things as they are." She swept her hand out, palm upward, signaling, *Everything's a mess out there*.

Dinah was interested to notice that even doing

emergency patrol work, Deputy Rosa Herrera had applied a cinnamon-red lipstick and blackish sparkly eyeliner. But Dinah also realized that her own enchantment at this was probably just relief that the deputies weren't looters. Or worse.

Nice eyeliner, though, that didn't run in a three-day hurricane! That must be Deputy Herrera's way of cheering herself up.

"I'm not moving these kids over there," said Gage in a growly, more grown-up tone than he usually used. "Are you nuts? We'll take our chances here. Besides, if their folks get through, they'll come here. They'll expect to find us here."

Deputy Campbell shone the light right in Gage's face, making him blink. "Son, if you're not a legal guardian, then I can't leave you with these kids. You're clearly not in control of the situation if you're letting the boy loose to break into homes and loot—"

"Mrs. Golightly is a neighbor," Zeke interrupted hotly. "She wouldn't mind. The law of charity."

"What about the law of sanity? We're wasting time here," said Deputy Campbell.

Deputy Herrera turned to Gage. "Look, mister, we got a drop in the wind for an hour, more or less. So most of our gang is up on Pilot's Knob seeing if they can get the transformer fixed before the wind returns. Or if not fixed, at least slap up a tarp and a wind shield to allow work to continue after the storm ramps up again. Yeah, it's gonna."

She sounds, thought Dinah, *as if she is about to spit in disgust. It must be hard to do her job.*

In any case, the woman continued. "We're in the eye of the storm now. The witching hour. But it's coming back, at least a couple more hours of bluster before dawn. Maybe it'll calm down then. But if the mudslides continue, nobody and her sister's gonna get to Pilot's Knob for another few days yet. According to the National Weather Service. Mount Raparus is a mess too, they say."

"*Is* there still a National Weather Service?" This was Zeke, trying to sound sardonic and grown-up, thought Dinah. But she could hear the worry in his voice.

Deputy Herrera ignored him. "Look, we can't stay here chewing the fat and we can't let you all stay here either, for your own good. Specially if Mister Teenager isn't the legal guardian."

"I'm a cousin of their mother," said Gage. "I'm twenty-one. Not a minor. Employed full-time. Language arts teacher, as it happens. Visiting from upstate."

"The parents cleared out and left you in charge?" Deputy Campbell looked dubious. "Not such a smart choice, seeing you're not up to the job."

"There was a—situation," said Gage. "Their

mother panicked. You improvise in a crisis. As we all know. So maybe I fell asleep an hour ago, a little bit." (Dinah realized that the same must be true for her, too.) "Long enough for Zeke to slip out," Gage admitted. "But look, he's a good fellow—just a little antsy. Who could blame him? We're doing fine here. Now don't dawdle on our account. You go on and help those who really need it."

"Mister," said Deputy Herrera in a voice that said *nonnegotiable*: "either *you* pick up that baby or *I* do."

But Gage had had enough. "You're not going to wake up a toddler in the middle of the night; you know better than that. Do you really think she'd get any sleep at some emergency shelter? Look, I heard the news before the power cut out. I know what conditions are like at the shelter. I'm not bringing these kids, whether they're mine or not, over there. I'm just not."

"Besides," said Dinah, "I won't go."

"Dinah," said Zeke wearily, as if this little snafu were all her fault instead of all his.

She looked at him. Her big brother, the good one in the lineup! Running away, no less. Breaking and entering. He appeared ashamed of himself, his chin tucked down into the dripping collar of his jacket. He looked bigger, too. Pity he got caught, thought Dinah, impressed despite herself.

She kept on. "I won't go. I won't. Gage is right

– 158 –

in the middle of his story, and we won't be able to hear it over there, what with the gunshots and the gang violence and the hymn singing."

Addressing the adults, Gage cut in. "I've got an idea. We have a generator, but it's on the fritz. If we're in a lull, maybe you can help me get it up and running. With a little light in the darkness—well, you know—"

"Don't go meaningful on me; don't have the time," said Deputy Campbell. "Sure, we can go have a look. Because a house with a working generator on this side of the district would be a godsend. We could use this place as a safe house while we're ferrying other holdouts and weirdos outta here. But get one thing straight. Fixed generator or no, I'm not giving you permission to stay, got that? No how, no way, José. You're coming with us. Now show me where the useless pile of junk is, will you?"

Gage shrugged himself into a jacket. Deputy Herrera said, "I'll babysit."

"We don't need sitters; we're not babies," snapped Dinah.

Deputy Herrera indicated Zeke. "You need jailers, then. I'll mind the jail." She took out a lipstick and attended to matters.

The men went out into the beguiling and unusual stillness.

"So where are your folks?" asked Deputy

Herrera, snapping her lipstick closed and stifling a yawn.

Zeke signaled to Dinah that she shouldn't give anything away.

Dinah was smart enough to figure that out for herself. But she was torn. Here was a chance to learn what was really going on out there—what part was storm, what part was earthquake, what part was human panic and rampage? Once the news had stopped broadcasting, Gage had stopped musing aloud. He was treating the whole disaster as if it were a picnic on a desert island.

But still, she reasoned quickly, she'd rather stay on a desert island with her relatives than get deported to an overcrowded shelter on the cutthroat mainland.

So she said to Deputy Herrera, "Look, I have to catch Zeke up on the story. If he's been out roaming the neighborhood, he's missed out on what happened to the skibberee."

"A skibbydoo? A dosey-do? What's a skibberee?"

"That's the formal scientific name of the creature we call a tooth fairy," Dinah explained. She sat down officiously and put on her best girl's-club manner. Imitating Brittney and Juliette as well as she could, she folded her legs beneath her, leaned her chin in her hands, pressed her elbows against her knees. She talked in that exaggerated, singsongy, know-it-all way that her downslope friends always did. "You *think* you know about tooth fairies, but, hel-*loooo:* you really *don't.*"

"What I don't know about cavities!" said Deputy Herrera. "I could write the book about root canals. It would be a horror story and outsell Stephen King." She lowered herself to the floor and leaned against the arm of the sofa. "So you know the Tooth Fairy personally?"

"There isn't just one," said Dinah. "Think about it: how could there be? Hundreds of children losing their teeth every day? A single tooth fairy could *never* manage the assignment. So there are whole *tribes* of them. Colonies. Flocks of them. Arranged in sectors and divisions and stuff. They live underground in hollowed-out trees, mostly where those highway ramps circle around. The talented ones are the tooth fairies the way we think of them, flying around with money and collecting the dead teeth. Agents of Change, they're called. Others stay in the colony and—well, I don't know what they do there. Gage didn't tell us yet."

"So did What-the-Dickens end up at a colony?" asked Zeke.

"Were you gone for that long?" asked Dinah, and then she realized he was giving her a hint: talk on. Sure enough, Deputy Herrera's eyelids were low—she must have been up several nights running, with limited chance for rest. "He did," she said, downshifting to a softer volume. "Pepper took Claire's baby tooth back to the Undertree Common, somewhere near Fern Hill, and What-the-Dickens followed along. There he met Old Flossie, the stump mistress, and Doctor Ill, the boss. But they were late arriving, and Pepper got—what's the word—demerits—she got penalized, that's it, for being late. She had to take What-the-Dickens out and lose him for good. Then she had one last chance to complete a mission on time. Which she wasn't pleased about."

"Really?" said Zeke.

"Oh, well, tooth fairies go it alone, you know. You don't see gangs of tooth fairies roaming the night skies like flying monkeys or anything. There's safety in numbers, sure, but there's another kind of safety in working solo. So Pepper is ticked off that she was late because of running into What-the-Dickens. Who is pretty clueless, even if he's got a good heart. And he follows her out of Doctor Ill's office, and is she asleep yet?"

"She's out," said Zeke in a low voice. There was a soft snore from Deputy Herrera to prove it.

"Look what you've done." Dinah used the same singsong voice, but she frowned at Zeke. "They're going to cart us away, and then even if Dad's Subaru *manages* to get overland and come back for us, we won't be here. We'll be stuck in some stinky air-less gymnasium with everyone else. What were you thinking of?"

"I went to see if I could find some cake for Rebecca Ruth's birthday," said Zeke.

Dinah raised her eyebrows. Wow. "You're a good big brother," she had to concede. "Good, brave, and stupid. Your bright idea has just cost us our freedom. Did you find any cake?"

He grinned for the first time in days. He said, "I left it in the breezeway. It's gummy and gross. It must have been defrosting and refreezing as the power came on and off. But it can't have gone bad yet. We can smooth out the frosting with a spoon in the morning and put your little candle in it. It'll do."

"The world is going down the tubes and you've risked *your* life and *our* liberty to get your baby sister a birthday cake." Dinah shook her head. "I'm tempted to say that just about takes the cake, but you already took it."

"Hah, hah."

"Well, I have to give you some credit. You snuck out without Gage or me noticing. We must've been nodding off. But the cake isn't going to go very far if we have to share it with four hundred people at the shelter."

Zeke nodded. "Don't think we have much choice now."

"We're not going to the shelter," said Dinah. "We're not being moved. We're staying here until—well, you know. Until Dad and Mom get back—or until we hear—something. We have to."

"How're we going to manage that?" said Zeke.

Dinah said, "Now listen: You got the cake, so I'll handle the next campaign. Quiet down and give me a chance to think. Gage and the geezer deputy will be back any minute."

She chewed the ends of her hair and looked around the living room at the blankets, at sleeping Rebecca Ruth, at the guttering candle. Did Deputy Herrera have a gun? Could two kids lift it off her and use it to bluff their way out of this mess? Not likely. Too risky. Deputy Herrera's arms were folded across her bosom, for one thing. If she had a shoulder holster on, it was hidden underneath her rain slicker.

Use your good mind, her dad always said. So Dinah tried to think in her usual *What've-we-got-here?* fashion:

- The storm outside was resting, not over. It was taking a break. It was at intermission.
- The evacuations weren't voluntary anymore. What was the word? Forced. Bossed. Mandatory.
- The deputies didn't like kids roaming around alone.

But somewhere in there, hardly a separate point but more a general background noise, something else figured in:

♦ For their own safety, those skibbereen stayed hidden, and they were forbidden to show themselves.

Then Dinah had an idea. She could even see where it came from: by overlaying a story notion atop the way the world was working on this most peculiar night.

She told it to Zeke and gave him cues on how to play it. "You're going to have to be convincing," she whispered. "You're going to have to lie. I know how much you hate to do that, but there's no other choice."

"Act like I'm terrifed? I can be convincing at that," he said. "I've been practicing that for most of this week. As for lying—I'll deal with that in my own conscience. It's none of your business. Get on, if you're going; she might wake up any second."

Dinah flicked her eyes this way and that. Quietly she slipped into the shadows between the sloping back of the sofa and the front door, up against which the threadbare thing had been lodged. From there, she could hear everything.

When Gage and Deputy Campbell returned in a few moments, Deputy Herrera jerked herself awake and yawned. "Coulda stayed like that till morning—morning the day after tomorrow," she groaned. Dinah pictured her getting up stiffly and rubbing the small of her back. "Any luck with the generator, Frank?"

"No. Not my field of expertise, I'm afraid," said the voice of Deputy Campbell. "So, come on now, better wrap that young 'un up against the winds, which are gonna rev up again within the hour. We have a small window of opportunity in which to get you safely down to the shelter. Let's shake a leg, now."

"Come on, Zeke," said Gage. His voice was low. "I guess there's nothing else to do. We held out for as long as we could."

"We can't go," said Zeke.

Dinah guessed that Deputy Campbell was aiming the beam of light in Zeke's face, trying to smoke out the meaning behind those words.

"It's my fault," said Zeke. His voice sounded softer, embarrassed. *Good job,* thought Dinah. "My lousy example. Dinah got the idea from me, I guess. She lit out herself. I don't know where she went."

"She didn't," said Deputy Herrera. "My eyes were closed only a second!"

The flashlights poked at the corners of the room, and Deputy Herrera then left to make a swift circuit of the small house. "I don't be-*lieve* it!" she railed from a bedroom, slamming a closet door. "You people *want* to get yourselves killed? Is *that* it?"

Dinah heard Gage say nothing—*he must be just standing there like a goon. A bodyguard, dumb and unblinking.*

Deputy Herrera wouldn't let it go. "You know a couple of folks got electrocuted by stepping on a downed power line, the only live line still left in the whole godforsaken *county*?" Her voice was shrill, nearly teary.

"It's my fault," Zeke mumbled again and again. "I'm sorry."

In the end, the exhausted deputies had no choice. They couldn't take Gage away, for if Dinah returned to the house when the storm picked up, she'd need to find an adult there. The deputies also couldn't take Zeke and Rebecca Ruth with them—not without Gage to protect them. The safety shelter clearly wasn't as safe as all that.

So they gave Gage a couple of candy bars and two extra D-cell batteries for his flashlight. "You got no food, no power, no working phone," harrumphed Deputy Herrera. "Two candy bars aren't going to last you long."

"We've been fine so far," said Gage helpfully. "Thanks for looking in on us."

They wished him luck brusquely and then tramped back out into the night.

Dinah listened to the silence return to the room. Gently she felt the lining of the back of the sofa; it was ripped, as if mice had eaten a doorway and crawled inside. *Stay safe in there, you guys,* she thought to them. *Don't get blown to kingdom come.*

"Salt of the earth, those two deputies," said Gage. "God keep them, as your mother would say. We ran those good souls ragged, Zeke, and that was totally unnecessary. They're going to drop in their tracks. Now: where is your blasted sister? If she's hiding somewhere outside, she'd better come back in again. The winds'll pick up any moment."

It was happening even as he spoke. A sound of tidal fury, only made of surging air and roiling rain, not seawater.

Dinah didn't want Gage to be frightened for her, but she kept hidden a while longer, just in case the deputies were watching through the window. Finally, though, her leg started falling asleep. She had to move and rustle. In an instant her face was raked by the beam from the flashlight. Gage, his face stony, jerked his thumb at her: *Get outta there, you.*

"Well, that's that." Dinah efficiently shifted attention to her brother. "All I can say is, good one, Zeke. You almost got us busted."

"I got us the birthday cake," said Zeke.

"And I got us out of the emergency shelter," said Dinah. "So we're even."

"You kids are nuts," said Gage. Relieved to have them united again, his voice grew harsher. "Horsing around this late. Scaring me half to death, Zeke! If you were my kid I'd wallop you something good."

"I'm not," said Zeke. "And I got the cake, didn't I?"

They glared at each other. Gage clenched and unclenched his fist. He breathed several times, then continued in a steadier tone. "You got the cake. Give you that much. Now it's the witching hour already, the darkest bit before dawn. Are you two finally ready to settle down and get some real sleep?"

"Are you kidding?" said Dinah. "I'm wider awake than ever. This is starting to be a test, isn't it? Like an Outward Bound kind of thing. Can we stay awake all night long? This has got to be the darkest night, doesn't it?—They're working on the transformer, they said; surely by tomorrow things will get back to normal?"

"Tomorrow," said Gage. He lay flat on his back and squeezed his eyes closed for a moment. "Tomorrow, and tomorrow, and tomorrow . . . O brave new world, That has such people in't! Though

I conflate, to make a point. Well, we'll see. To quote another genius, 'Tomorrow is another day.' "

Zeke stuffed his face in a pillow and pretended to scream.

"Don't you ever get tired of quoting?" asked Dinah.

"No," said Gage, sitting up again. "Like a visit from Deputy Herrera and Deputy Campbell, quoting reminds me there are other people in the world besides only me. And other thoughts besides mine, and other ways of thinking."

"There are," agreed Dinah. "Namely, Pepper. Her next assignment. Her punishment: she has to take What-the-Dickens on a tooth run and lose him for good. In the wild. Isn't that where you were headed?"

"Aren't you worn out?" asked Gage.

"You tell such a good story," Dinah said, wheedling.

"You do a pretty good job yourself, you," said Gage. "Well, come closer. The wind is getting louder, and I don't want to risk waking Rebecca Ruth up now, not when she's managed to sleep through our unexpected company."

Gage put his arms around Zeke and Dinah. If either of them tried to wriggle away again, he'd know it.

The Tooth Fairy Bites Back

❧ FOURTEEN ❧

So, you do remember where we were?

What-the-Dickens and Pepper were hustling along the corridors of—the colony.

Right: Undertree Common. Northwest Sector, Division B. Good listening.

The skibbereen were heading for the bank. In a hurry. And in states of mind alike in some ways, not alike in others.

The orphan skibberee had lost his grin. The impact of Doctor Ill's pronouncement was beginning to hit home. *Hah,* thought What-the-Dickens, *hit home. Such as I've ever known, for one full night of my life.*

But Pepper has been given another chance to earn her right to roam—away from home now and then—and this is good. Since it was my fault she reported in late, I should just be quiet. Let her succeed, and accept my own banishment. So I almost had a home? Let it go. If I can.

No, not if. I must let it go. I will.

Still, What-the-Dickens resented the bossiness of Doctor Ill. Why should the crown have all the say in whether Pepper could become an Agent of Change? Which meant whether she could be a "named" skibberee instead of an anonymous worker-citizen.

To distract himself from his sour ponderings, he asked, "Why are we going to the bank?"

Pepper explained as they hurried along. "Skibbereen—tooth fairies, as they're called nowadays—don't steal. Everything is strictly on the up-and-up, no funny business. If we want a tooth, we buy it. We take it and we leave the payment behind."

"What kind of payment?" asked What-the-Dickens.

"The best kind. Cash," said Pepper. "Cash is both pretty and portable."

"But where do you get it?"

"Where do you think? We mine it."

"You mine it? It comes out of the ground all clean and newly minted?"

"Hardly new," said Pepper, "but true coin don't lose its value over time the way, say, baloney does. You see, every colony develops a group of skibbereen called the Scavengers. They're like diviners who can find water with a forked branch of hickory wood. After scads and scads of years, Scavengers have evolved to be able to smell the presence of metal in the dirt. They go on foraging trips almost every night. Those trips ain't as dangerous as the trips that we Agents of Change make, for *we* have to skootch right up close to the dread human creature, whereas Scavengers only go where humans have already *been*."

She said we. *She thinks of herself as an Agent of Change already. She wants that so badly.* "What sorts of places do Scavengers go?" he continued.

"Oh, here, there. Playgrounds, for instance. A lot of spare change grows in the dirt underneath a jungle gym. Used car lots, too. At night Scavengers investigate the latest trade-ins. You'd be amazed how much moola can be found in the cracks between the seat cushions. Also pay phones. Also places with views, what human colonies sometimes calls Lovers' Lanes. Rich with possibility!"

"But that's stealing," said What-the-Dickens. "*Isn't* that stealing?"

"Oh, no, not at all," demurred Pepper. "True, we take the poor lost nickels and quarters and even dollar coins, and we clean them up. But we don't keep them for good. We give them a nice new home under the pillow of some child who has just lost a tooth.

Besides, don't you know, we pay for the money. We trade something back to humans for all the money we get from them. We're in the tooth trade. It's our *economy*."

"What do you—do we—give for the money we find?" But was it *you* or *we*?

"Later," said Pepper. "Here's the bank."

She stopped before a pair of gates hung in the walls of the corridor. Each gate was made of colored wooden beads strung horizontally on iron rods fixed into a polished wooden frame. "Getting the Gates of Abacus installed was quite an achievement," said Pepper proudly. "It's a bit over the top, but this is a temple to currency and we like to keep current. Clea, I'm here for my disbursement."

A skibberee lurking behind a rank of bright red beads pushed aside a bead to peer at them. Clea the Banker. She sported a pair of fuzzy spectacles fashioned out of pipe cleaners. Perhaps she wore them to make herself appear smart. *But she looks ridiculous,* thought What-the-Dickens, as he remembered the spectacles on Granny Menace's mantelpiece. Clea's glasses were three sizes too large and had no lenses.

"Oooooh," said Clea, pushing aside several more beads so she could get a better look, "who's this you got with you, Pepper? A boyfriend?"

"A *friend,*" said Pepper, "and it's none of your business."

"A friend who's a boy," said Clea.

"No, I'm a boy who's a friend," said What-the-Dickens. "I was a boy first and a friend second."

"Not the rogue tooth fairy I've been hearing about?" Clea was scandalized. She reared back onto her behind, then stood up, took off her glasses and pretended to clean the lenses on her wing tips so she could see him better. "My word! It is! What is he doing here?"

"I got an assignment, Clea. And I'm kinda like in a hurry? I can't discuss it now. Open up."

"But Doctor Ill would never assign a rogue tooth fairy to accompany an Agent of Change!" remarked Clea. She hesitated at the latch. "Pepper, are you in cahoots with a bad element? We haven't had a bank robbery here for one or two or what-comes-next months. Or years. This is terribly irregular. I'll have to get some confirmation—"

"We've met the crown. We're on assignment," Pepper advised her briskly. "If *you* want to be kicked out of your position and be sent back down to the field, Clea, dither away. Be my guest. Maybe that'll open a position in the bank for my friend here, who's looking for work, I bet."

"I don't have a good feeling about this," Clea remarked, though she began to unlatch the gates as she spoke. "If we don't know your friend's background, we can't possibly know what he's good for. We each have a calling. It would be criminal to send out a homebody Harvester to do the job of an Agent of Change. They'd get all muddled and end up squished flat on some automobile windshield like your common moth."

"What-the-Dickens doesn't know his own strength," said Pepper calmly. "But in any case, Doctor Ill makes those calls, not you, Clea. *Will* you hurry a bit?"

"Quite right, quite right." Clea clucked to herself. "I stand corrected. I'm only the banker. Now, what can I get you, Pepper dear?"

Pepper didn't answer. She led What-the-Dickens through the gates into a chamber luminous with gleam. The three interior walls of the vault (the Gates of Abacus made up the fourth) were built out of silvery metal. Shaped something like columns, they were embedded halfway into the walls. It all looked very rich, as the room was filled with the diffuse glow cast by lightning bugs housed within milkpod globes. A ten-dollar bill lay flat on the floor like a green area carpet.

"Wow," said What-the-Dickens. "This is grand."

"It's the most splendid bank I know of," said Clea proudly. "Also the only one. We call it the Only National Bank."

Pepper said to What-the-Dickens, "See, these are coin-changers used by human beings. Clea collects the funds that the Scavengers find and she stores them in these stacks. The money slots in at the top. By pushing against one of these levers down here at the bottom, she can get cash out, too—one coin at a time."

"How many coins do you have here?" asked What-the-Dickens.

Clea clucked. She rubbed her chin. She walked back and forth among the dozen or so columns of glittering coins—copper pennies, pewtery nickels, silvery dimes, rib-edged quarters.

"It's hard to get an accurate count," the

banker admitted. "Four? Or ninety? Somewhere in there."

"We can't stop to figure it out," said Pepper impatiently. "Besides, math is a myth. Doctor Ill always says so, and he knows. Clea, I just need a standard-issue quarter."

Clea walked back and forth across the room. She stroked her chin and occasionally took off her spectacles and chewed on the earpiece, which made it damp and disgusting.

"Hmmm," she said. "Hmmmm. Maybe? Yes. *Yes.* This one. I think you'll find this to your liking, my dear." Suddenly she bolted forward and threw herself against a lever at the floor level. A bright coin shot out like a metal Frisbee and caught What-the-Dickens in the ankle.

The skibberee examined it. On one side it was imprinted with a human head that seemed to have been severed from its body, for it ended at the neck. *Liberty,* read the coin. "Liberty for whom?" asked What-the-Dickens. "Not for her: she's been decapitated."

"Don't ask such nosy questions," said Clea.

"Don't mind him; he's a visitor," said Pepper.

"That's what I'm afraid of," replied Clea.

What-the-Dickens thought, *Afraid of a visitor? Afraid of someone who is your same shape and size and species and—sympathy?*

Or maybe not sympathy, he thought, looking at Clea's curled lip and lowered, calculating eyes.

Pepper lifted the quarter. For a skibberee, a coin like that is about the size of a large pizza. She inserted it vertically into her satchel, which latched closed thanks to some patches of burdock stitched in useful places—a kind of natural Velcro. "All right, Clea," she said. "I guess we're off."

"Pepper," said Clea. "Look. I want you to be careful, right? Going out in tandem is a risky, risky business. I don't know if Doctor Ill is punishing you or trusting you—but either way, you take care."

"It's not your business to question Doctor Ill," said Pepper sternly. She blew a little kiss at the banker, who pretended to catch it and then store it in a safe-deposit stack with some precious pennies.

The Gates of Abacus closed with a rattle of beads on rods. "Mind yourself, Pepper," said Clea.

What-the-Dickens noticed he was given no matching advice.

"Does she have a point?" asked What-the-Dickens. "Is this really safe?"

"Nothing is *safe*," said Pepper. "Not in the long run. We can't be safe and we can't be certain—but we can be careful, and we will."

"You're buzzing around the question," said What-the-Dickens. He stopped in the corridor. "I mean, why does the boss here have a name like Doctor Ill? Isn't that a bit, um, contradictory?"

"I told you, we all pick our names from the accidental scriptures," said Pepper, "but we change them so as not to be guilty of theft. Do the verbal math. *Pill* minus *P* is *Ill*. Get it?"

"Yes, but if you use an abbreviation for Doctor, then Doctor Ill is D.R. I.L.L. Drill."

"A basic dental term. So?"

"So he chose a nasty-sounding name. Is he a bully?"

"For shame," said Pepper. "You get thinking like that, and you'll lose your concentration and something bad will happen to you."

"I mean, that mouse," said the orphan skibberee. "In that muzzle and all."

FIFTEEN

"You didn't stand up for me very much," said What-the-Dickens.

"I don't know what you mean. Come on, we got a deadline to make."

"No." He stopped. "I stood by *you*, Pepper, at Doctor Ill's. I persuaded him to give you another chance. You could've been a little more—I don't know—a little less—what's the word—"

"Just because Clea thought you were a potential bank robber? Hah. *She* don't get around much."

"Well, maybe I am a potential bank robber," he said stubbornly, itching for a fight. "How do I know? How do *you* know unless you get to know me?"

"Don't talk like that!" She was alarmed; he could tell. Against the rules, she all but flew down the corridor toward the exit. Against the rules, he followed in like manner, his lumpen feet battering against the rustic trim that bedecked Undertree Common.

They emerged onto the landing strip—the top of the tree trunk—into a night brightened by a full moon.

"We don't have time to argue," said Pepper. "We're booked for the runway any minute."

"I'm not going," said What-the-Dickens.

"Oh, for pity's sake!"

"Why should I leave without even getting to know what life is really like here? That's just collaborating in my own banishment."

"Well, listen. *One:* I brought you here in the first place to look around, not to make trouble. *Another one:* You're overlooking that you're being *allowed* to leave. Like it is a given. And, to count out the reasons further, um, *five:* You owe me. You're the reason I almost missed out on my license. So quit all this malarkey, will you? Get a grip and let's get out of here."

All around the stump, they saw evidence of skibbereen activity. In loose formations, small groups of skibbereen were launching off the runway.

He hesitated. She looked so agitated. And he had no rights here. He was an alien.

"Okay," he said. "I yield to your common sense. But just show me a little bit more of the colony before we go, since I won't be coming back. I'd like to be able to picture where you live when I don't see you anymore."

"Don't talk like that!" she cried, horrified.

"Why not?"

"Because—because—skibbereen don't talk like that."

Oh, he thought. *Oh well. Right. Skibbereen are never seen—not even to each other.*

"Look," she said, caving in a little. "You have a point. Okay, I'll show you around some. We're in a holding pattern here anyway. These squadrons are leaving every few minutes; the full moon is a dandy time for them."

"I thought you didn't travel in packs," said What-the-Dickens.

"We Agents of Change don't," said Pepper. "Too risky. But those are the overnight delivery boys. They call themselves the Wish Team."

"What are they delivering?"

"Wishes. What else?"

"Pepper, I just don't get the commerce of all this. How *does* it work?"

"Listen up," said Pepper.

He looked about the place with the eagerness of a cub reporter at his first cafeteria food fight.

"A skibbereen colony is divided into two

sections," said Pepper, as if rattling off a school lesson. "Uppers and lowers. Most of us skibbereen are the lowers—the laborers. You got your Scavengers, remember, I already told you? They hunt for seed money to capitalize the trade. You got your Agents of Change, like me and many others; we're the solo operators on whom the tooth trade depends. We trade money for teeth. Then you got your Harvesters. *They* take the teeth we bring in and plant them, and tend them, and harvest them. You still with me?"

"You *plant* old teeth?"

"I don't—I'm an Agent of Change. Or I will be once I get my final license. But yes, we skibbereen do."

"But what do they grow into? More teeth?"

She looked at him in the moonlight. He thought her look was soft and sad. *It's not an easy time for her,* he realized. *Well, not for me either, but I notice it in her more. Just now.*

"I'll show you," she said impulsively. "Follow me. But move it."

They flew off the stump through a stand of tall grass. In the moonlight the growth stood out as stripes of ivory and sage against luminous black. Riblike, the blades arched above them.

"We double-plant," explained Pepper. "A whole field sown with teeth would draw attention to itself if it were ever discovered, so we inter-seed teeth with common grasses and weeds. Luckily a tooth grows to maturity in the space of one full-moony night. We harvest just before dawn, so human ramblers, even if they tramped their clod-footed way right through our fields, would never know the industry taking place beneath their hobnails and soccer cleats and stiletto heels."

"Show me!" What-the-Dickens was thrilled by all this secrecy and productivity. "I'm dying to know."

Pepper dropped to the ground. "Ladies?" she called. "Girls? Don't be scared; he's with me."

One by one, skibbereen females began to emerge from the forest of grass. They seemed, as a rule, shyer than the others, as if they didn't want to speak, as if they didn't like a male in their nursery. "He's new here," explained Pepper.

"What is he?" asked one of the less timid ones. "He doesn't look like a Scavenger." She bobbed and becked. You might say she looked like a tiny jellyfish, almost invisible in moonlight—insubstantial, and docile, and spineless.

"He's a mistake," said Pepper. She spoke without malice, but What-the-Dickens winced. A *mistake*? "He don't know what he is," Pepper continued, as if maybe she guessed at his discomfiture. "Doctor Ill don't know yet, either. Not a Harvester, though, dear ladies of the plantation, so don't stew your giddy heads over him. I'm just showing our guest the tooth garden. Won't be long. Settle down. You can go back to your tasks."

But the Harvesters hovered in a crowd, unwilling to separate. Murmuring like frightened doves.

Pepper sighed and whispered to her new friend, "They ain't got much character, poor chuckleheads, but they do give their all to their task." She pulled aside a decomposing leaf. Three tapered prongs were thrusting up from the ground—slender waxy posts of varying heights and thicknesses. One was about three-and-a-half inches tall and striped around with a pale, ascending blue line. "This one's about ready, I think," said Pepper. "Could one of you do the honors?"

But none of the Harvesters wanted to oblige.

"Very well, I'll do it myself," said Pepper. *"Really."* She reached down and snapped the narrow cylinder at its base. "I think this is done. See?"

She held it up. What-the-Dickens didn't recognize it.

"It's a birthday candle, for a birthday cake, silly," said Pepper. "Humans always blow on candles and make wishes on their birthdays, but the wishes only come true if they are made on one of *our* candles." Her voice was full of pride.

"Really? Wishes?" What-the-Dickens got all excited.

"Hey, wait," said Pepper. "I can see it on your face. Forget it. Tooth fairies don't get to wish. We're the *Agents* of Change, remember? We don't change *ourselves*. Ain't in the program! No wishing allowed."

"But I could wish to find my family!" he said.

"You might find that they were all dead," said Pepper frankly. "Anyway, you can't wish; it's not done. We work in the service of others, not ourselves."

At his hangdog look, Pepper took mercy. "Come on, now. Pay attention, okay? I'll review it for you. Scavengers collect the investment money. Agents of Change take each tooth and replace it with a coin. *Free the tooth!* Ha, ha. Then Harvesters plant the gathered teeth and tend the garden and reap the results on a full-moon night. Finally, the Wish Team flies our candles to the nearest stores or candle factories, or sometimes even to private homes, where we substitute one of ours for a commercially made candle. Most of our chores are done between midnight and dawn, because that's when the most humans are asleep. We call this the Wishing Hour."

"Joy," said What-the-Dickens, without much joy.

"Let's go," she said. "You'll feel better when we get to work. I always do."

They left the field of candles and made their way back through the grassy forest, on foot this time. "What about predators?" he said.

"Luckily," said Pepper, "we have few natural enemies in the wild. Sure, you have to watch out for the occasional nearsighted owl, who might mistake you for an airborne mouse. Then, of course, there's the dangerous deadly human."

"The ones we give *wishes* to?" He was aghast.

"You bet. Humans would pen us in cages and sell us as pets as soon as look at us, if they discovered us. The beasts. That's what they do. And human pets — like dogs and cats — are treacherous, like their owners. Probably goldfish would be, too, if goldfish could manage to get loose and roam the earth. They'd be schools of shiny assassins, I'm told. Vicious little creatures."

"But — giving wishes to humans — if it's so dangerous —"

"As a small, defenseless species goes, we make out all right." Pepper sounded offhand, but proud. "Cats are nocturnal, true, so that's an ongoing cause for alarm. But our only serious natural enemy is ourselves."

"Meaning . . . ?"

"The separate colonies of skibbereen ain't always able to live in peace and tranquility. Sometimes there are raids, and the occasional Harvester or Scavenger gets carried off. I've known bank robberies you wouldn't believe. Now and again, an outright attack. An invasion. There's a belligerent colony high up in a big old pine over near Pilot's Knob, called Sequoia Heights. Division D. You wouldn't want to mess around with them slobs, believe me."

"Does Undertree Common go on raids and attacks, too?"

"Depends on what the crown tells us to do. It ain't my business to decide on all that, is it? I'm an Agent of Change, or I will be if we ever get launched tonight. Let Doctor Ill decide whose Liberty is worth defending and whose Liberty is worth trespassing against."

"Why does he get to make all the decisions?"

"Oh, I didn't finish my little outline, did I?" They were nearing the runway on top of the stump, so Pepper dropped her voice, out of respect or, perhaps, caution.

"You see," she continued, "all that I described—the Scavengers, the Agents of Change, the Harvesters, and the Wish Team—that's us. We're lowers. The workers, that is. Anyone who is differentiated—well, you might say talented—they're uppers. Like Doctor Ill, and Old Flossie, et cetera. And Silviana the Entertainment Industry, and so on.

Clea the Banker. Not many of them, but they have harder work to do because they have to make it up themselves. The rest of us, we're more or less decided."

"What decides you—I mean us?"

"Instinct. And 'instinct breeds specialization.' They drill it into you in nursery school. I'm specialized to be a worker. An Agent of Change, who gets a dandy private name, is the highest I can hope to go. But uppers are specialized to be special. Look, uppers don't work unless they have something to grind against, and that's us: the lowers."

What-the-Dickens shook his head. It was all too confusing, mostly because he couldn't find himself in the scheme of things. "I don't know what I am, or what I was meant to be. A Harvester or an Agent of Change, a Scavenger or a member of the Wish Team."

"Nothing's better than being an Agent of Change," she said, forgetting for a moment to curb her excitement about it. "We get the most freedom, that is, within respectable limits. Look, are your wings unfurled? Let's stop yapping and get going. This is going to be a busy night."

But just when they turned to register with

the stump mistress and to queue up for take-off, a bunch of Wish Teamers cut the line and demanded priority clearance. And got it. "They think they're so smart," whispered Pepper, "but their brains are all in their bums. That's what gives them enough bottom, so to speak, to be able to haul a load of candles without being blown off course." Sure enough, the Wish Team fellows seemed broad of beam, fundamentally suited to carry the candles laced onto their backs with cords of knotted grass.

"I'm not built like that, either," said What-the-Dickens, "so I guess I'm not meant to be a member of the delivery services."

"Maybe you're a mutant," said Pepper cheerfully. "Another, I mean, if you believe the legend of the First Fairy. Now, your wings responding well enough?"

He looked at Pepper as she flexed her pair. Little specks of light ran in coded sequence along the tips, occasionally diverting along capillary routes back toward her shoulder blades. "How *does* all that work?" he marveled.

"Beats me," she said. "I'm not the brightest lightning bug in the storm cloud, you know. But our wings is our public access communications network. As whales sing headlines across the ocean depths, or elephants thump the news against dusty savannas, or songbirds twitter the daily gossip from tree to tree, we skibbereen receive information from Central Command through our wings. It's a kind of telegraphic system, I guess. We pick up changes in our assignments. Predator sightings, weather updates. That sort of thing."

"I can feel tingling, but I thought it was just pins and needles. It doesn't mean anything to me. How do you learn to read it?"

"You just *can*," she said. "Don't you do anything by instinct?"

"Ask questions?" he said, not as a joke. "Does that qualify?"

"Well, stop asking," she replied. "We're being signaled out for departure. Good luck, friend."

Old Flossie squinted at the moon, counted on her fingers several times—one, one—one, one—counted What-the-Dickens and Pepper—one, one—and gave up. "Higher math," she muttered. "Twists my noggin into pretzels something dreadful. Math is a myth. Okay, you-all over there. Oh, it's Pepper. And What's-His-Name."

"What-the-Dickens," he corrected her.

"Whatever-the-Dickens. So this is good-bye, then," said Old Flossie. "I'm not much for sentiment, but I wish you the best. You're not a spy, we decided that, so you're just a raw nerve. Here's my parting advice to you, since you come unequipped with sense of any sort. Keep hidden. Got that? And if you're ever caught, go to your grave with our secret on your lips. Squealing is forbidden. *You* are forbidden. Got it?"

"What if I'm tortured?"

"Ask no questions," barked Old Flossie, out of habit, and continued, "and don't answer any, either."

He nodded, catching her murmured remark to herself as she turned away, "And don't come back, fellow, if you know what's good for you."

"Ready for countdown," said Pepper, positioning herself.

"Three," said Old Flossie, "four, six, go on, get outta here."

Pepper tucked her head down to correct against possible wind shear, and What-the-Dickens tried to do the same. There was still so much to learn. First and foremost, though, was the basic matter of whether he was even capable of learning anything.

"Go, I said," shouted Old Flossie. So they did.

❧ ❧ ❧

"Well, it's a good thing you got that birthday cake, isn't it?" said Dinah, when Gage had paused to go to the bathroom. "We can put that birthday candle in it and see if it's one of the wishing ones." She rummaged around in the fireplace and found it.

"I certainly don't believe in wishes," said Zeke. "I hardly believe in the cake, at this point."

"Hah," said Dinah. "What would Rebecca Ruth wish for, I wonder?"

"Better cake, I bet."

Gage came back. "I haven't been able to lull you to sleep, I see," he said.

"When are you coming into this story?" asked Dinah.

"You just don't let go, do you?" he answered her. "Oh, well, I guess there's nothing to do but move on. The next bit's about me. A little."

SIXTEEN

Carefully watching Pepper launch into the west, What-the-Dickens picked up a few more tips about skibbereen aerial maneuvers. Bit by bit, his flying skills were improving. He saw how much energy he'd spent floundering, pumping those fragile wings like a butterfly in a tornado. Now he could harness the wind a little better, coast a little longer, and conserve his energy.

The moon throbbed like candleglow behind very thin clouds—it kept its shape as a heavenly coin, but the light melted out in skirts all around it.

Suddenly the language of the night—the way winds never stop, really, even on the stillest of still evenings—came clear to the orphan skibberee. The world was constantly talking to itself, in remarks and replies, in choruses and antiphons. What was the noise a tree could make but the noise a wind made in it? And with his wings, What-the-Dickens himself shaped a slender hollow in the night. He was a reed whispering its own small testimony to the world, and about it.

He might have talked to Pepper—she was that near—but she seemed disinclined to chatter, and he couldn't blame her. Even dreading his eventual good-bye to Pepper—maybe because that good-bye hadn't happened yet—this evening's flight was the best example of happiness he'd come across yet. The world below was purple and crumpled, broken up into clumps of houses and trees, fields and barns. The air aloft was shot with bevels of warm and cold. It smelled of earth and nothing else. The stars were mostly hidden; the moon was a ghostly galleon tossed upon cloudy seas. It was pretty.

All too soon Pepper flicked one wing tip, signaling her intention to descend into society. What-the-Dickens followed, gracelessly, but not without a certain oomph.

He still couldn't figure out how Pepper's wings informed her about her position and destination. Maybe his wings weren't wired right . . . or maybe they were wired for a different task entirely.

He thought, I *wouldn't have known to begin to sink right here, over this simple unrenovated farmhouse. Its pleasant boxy shape, its lack of architectural gewgaw, its softly steaming chimney—it says nothing to me that the houses farther down the road don't also say.*

But there Pepper was headed, and so he

was headed there, too. Sticking close to her. Until. Until.

Nearer the earth, the winds were stronger—why was that? The skibbereen went back to flying *en pointe,* as it were, with a certain amount of attitude. The traditional angelic pose: leading with your right shoulder, your nose, and your brow, and letting your legs trail along for the ride rather than pumping them.

The skibbereen whipped once around the house. Pepper, apparently, was looking for a way to enter. She was flummoxed though, and wagged a finger, indicating that they regroup on top of a mailbox by the road. "This stinks," said Pepper. "I'm supposed to say good-bye to you here, then slip inside and do my work alone. But the place is sealed up tighter than Croesus's safe-deposit box. What gives? It's the rare farmhouse that don't leave a window open a crack, even in the bitterest winter. Farmers like fresh air."

"Maybe they're not farmers. Who are we looking for?"

"Who am *I* looking for," Pepper corrected him, a bit sternly. "This is our sad farewell, but let's make it snappy. I got to find a way in."

"I'll stay till I can't any longer," he said.

"If you argue, you're wasting your own time, and you don't have that much of it left. We both don't," he finished. "I mean, you and me together. Now, tell me the contact information."

"You don't have *any* of this on your roster?" Pepper shook her head sadly. "They posted the details all across the colony network. There's something radically busted with your reception, buddy."

"There's something wrong," he agreed, "but let's not obsess about me. Who is our client?"

"It's a boy kid," she said, "named Gage. Gage Tavenner. He's had a pesky little incisor waiting to come out for weeks. Our best information says he fell backward off his chair at breakfast and knocked out the little beauty at last. So my job is to nip in there, nab the goods, pay the tribute, and get out. Once I can find a way in, that is."

"We'll manage it," he said, liking the sound of that hopefulness.

"Now you listen to me, What-the-Dickens," said Pepper. "Butt out. I can't afford to be late getting back. My whole license depends on executing this maneuver in a timely fashion, and—wait; what's that?"

She screwed up her forehead as if listening to a wireless. "Incoming . . ." she whispered, and made a *shhh*-ing gesture.

What-the-Dickens saw her wings flick in sequins of slightly different colors—first, silvery beads like rain on a spiderweb; next, silver interspersed with a smoky yellow; and then silver accented with a mouthwash blue. "Oh, great," she moaned. "I might've guessed."

"What?" he said. "What?"

"They have it in for me," she said. "Always did, you know! Think I'm too—oh, I don't know. Opinionated. Loud. Not classy enough. *Common*. Now getta load of this: they've doubled my assignment. They're claiming a dental emergency. Nearby, a tooth from someone named Lee Gangster. What a name! I gotta wrap this job up fast and get way out to Gangsterland. And what am I supposed to use for tribute? I only brought one coin."

"Maybe I was supposed to bring one," said What-the-Dickens.

"Maybe you were," she snapped. "Maybe they were telling you so on your wing set, and you *didn't read your instructions*."

"I'm sorry."

"Well, first things first. Gotta get this one

over with. Ought to be a walk in the park once I get in. How to crack the site, though?"

"Look," said What-the-Dickens. Pepper turned, but she didn't see what he had seen—the flick of shadowy gray—something—disappearing off the back porch and into—a hatch? A small door? "Follow me," he said.

He led her around the side of the house, and they examined what they had previously overlooked. "What is it?" asked What-the-Dickens.

"It's called a cat flap," said Pepper. "And call me a genius, but where there's a cat flap there is usually a cat."

"There was," he said. "I saw the last bit of one disappear inside. It was indistinct in the shadows. But I know it's in there."

"From bad to worse," she groaned. "This is a trap. They've set me an impossible task. They don't want me to come back alive."

"Pepper," he said, and tugged at her wing so hard that she yelped. "I'll come in with you. If the cat sniffs you out, I'll distract it. I know cats. Firsthand, and from the beginning. Use the help you have on hand. *Me*. Come on, let's go."

He pushed ahead of her, breathing hard—surprised at himself—and leaned on the small door. "Are you coming?" he said over his shoulder, and Pepper followed without speaking.

The house was orderly to a fault. The rooms were strict in their arrangements: chairs lined up along the wall of the dining room like soldiers, spaced evenly apart. In the moonlight the table surfaces gleamed like lakes of mahogany. No books anywhere; books were such dreadful dust collectors. On the wallpapered walls a few browned photographs of pinched-looking relatives hung in oval frames. They looked like portals from beyond the grave. It seemed even dead folk could still manage to disapprove.

Sane. Antiseptic. The wrong type of peculiar.

"Does your radar tell you exactly where the tooth is?" asked What-the-Dickens in a hush. "I'm not picking up a thing."

"No. You got to apply a certain amount of common sense, which in your case, I'm realizing, ain't all that common. A human don't usually sleep in a dining room—let's check out the kitchen. Farmhouses of a certain age often got a spare bedroom off the kitchen, for a farm maid to use, or a granny who needs to sleep nearer the stove for warmth. Or an extra kid. Stick close, you hear me?"

He nodded. They achieved the kitchen, an homage to sterility and order, from its squares of red-and-white linoleum to its Agway farm calendar, a blue ink slash striking out those days of the month already lived into submission and buried in memory: even yesterday.

"There's no bedroom off here," said What-the-Dickens.

"No cat, either," said Pepper. "Cats often hug the stove light, too. Are you sure you saw something entering?"

"I think I did. It's why my eye veered to the back porch."

"We'll have to go even more slowly. All right, let's move out."

They circled through the formal parlor, where on a side table a hand-carved chess set was displayed. It was so neatly set that it looked as if no one was allowed to play with it. What-the-Dickens wanted to pet the mane of the knight's piece, which was carved like a horse's head, but he could see by the look in Pepper's eye that he had better just shadow her.

They caught a slight draft of heated air eddying up the stairwell to the second floor. Several doors gave out onto a landing. One was a bathroom with a night-light, and that door was slightly open. Other doors were open, too, a few inches each. Pepper's intincts said the door on the left, and her instincts were wrong—there was a smell of sour adult breath—so then they tried the door on the right.

Gage was sleeping in his bed. He was an only kid—only and lonely, both, because his parents had other obligations besides child rearing, and reminded him about this on a daily basis. He couldn't have brothers or sisters, they told him: life was tough and he should just get on with it.

His room was spare, like the downstairs rooms—not so much as a comic book collection, or baseball cards, or drawings taped up on the walls—the tape would leave marks, he was told—or books. Only a desk with his homework ready for the morning. Stacked on the paper blotter.

"He's a solid sleeper—I can tell by the way his adenoids are whistling," whispered Pepper. "Let's hope he's not a deadweight on the pillow. Those are the worst. You got to tickle them exactly right, enough to make them stir but not enough to awaken them. It's a dicey business and the first place that things can go very, very wrong."

"Why can't you just wake him up and do this transaction in public?" asked What-the-Dickens.

She shot him a look. "And be seen? And be caught? And be caged? And be sold? And maybe be tortured? And betray our colony? And our mission? And deprive the world of the possibility of wishes that really *might* come true? What kind of world do you *want* to live in, anyway? That's the big question, ain't it?"

"I thought you said to *shhh*," he answered, cowed by her intensity and ashamed of his own ignorance.

She led him to the mattress. They landed gently on the edge of the sheet. Gage's head was turned toward the wall, so at least they weren't in danger of his suddenly opening his eyes and seeing them.

Pepper tugged at the pillow, looking for the tooth. It was a heavily compacted pillow made out of duck feathers. That sort doesn't have the airy bounce of its foam rubber cousin, but tends to flop at rest as if exhausted by its own muscular weight.

The skibbereen both began to burrow, but they had to beware of suffocation. Then, too, there was the slim chance that, while they were halfway under the pillow, the sleeper would roll over and crush them.

After a while, having no luck, What-the-Dickens turned and stood with his spine against the pillow and tried to walk backward, inching the pillow up along his wings to widen the space between pillow and sheet. It was hard work, and dangerous, but he managed well enough for Pepper to dive face-first into the linens.

She scissored her arms back and forth in the dark seam. By the digging in of her knees, What-the-Dickens could tell that Pepper had found something. She was reaching for a fingerhold of the buried treasure when the bedroom door cracked open an extra inch.

The strip of light from the upstairs hall widened.

What-the-Dickens was facing the door. He couldn't move, or he'd risk killing Pepper by the collapse of the heavy pillow. But he could see what was approaching.

Who was approaching.

"Look!" he shouted—he couldn't help himself. His heart fizzed and sputtered and his eyes watered. He felt less like the *mistake* that Pepper had called him and more like a miracle.

Gage stirred at the noise; Pepper panicked and came up at a clip, hugging the tooth. "Look," said What-the-Dickens again. "It's impossible. It's McCavity."

⚹ ⚹ ⚹

"I don't get it. What was McCavity doing there?" asked Dinah.

"McCavity was my cat," said Gage. "I guess I hadn't told you that part yet."

They thought about it. "So your home wasn't all *that* chilly, if you could have a cat," said Zeke.

"Yes, well," said Gage, "but, I mean, really: *McCavity*? Not especially your coziest specimen of cat, as cats go. Vain, self-centered, and aggressive. Hardly a boy's best friend. Still, she was mine: my responsibility. I had begged for a pet and begged for a pet, and she was my punishment for all that begging."

"If your parents were so mean, how'd you learn to be nice?" asked Dinah.

"That's how," he explained.

"Hey," said Zeke, figuring it out. "McCavity was your cat, so you were the one who picked her up and shook the skibberee out of the old tin can. Right?"

"Looks like it, doesn't it?" said Gage.

Dinah thought two things almost at the same time:

+ Gage
+ Gage

Only the first one was Gage at ten, and the second was Gage at twenty-one and a half—the Gage stifling yet another yawn as Dinah studied him in the shadows.

"Then you were the one who gave What-the-Dickens his name," said Dinah at last.

"Bingo," said Gage.

❧ SEVENTEEN ❧

Pepper froze for only an instant, and then, as she jettisoned herself in the air a foot above the bed, she whispered, "Scoot!" Not to the cat, but to What-the-Dickens.

The weight of the pillow rested on the orphan skibberee's shoulders, and so he had to inch forward slowly. But he was in no hurry, either. Once he got out, he scrambled to the edge of the bed.

He no longer thought that McCavity would understand his words—that was yet another mistake of his very recent and silly youth. Still, in the presence of that furry face, in the gleam of her calibrating eyes, he felt compelled to speak. "McCavity, I once hoped to be your pet. I hoped I could buy my way into your heart with a perfect present. I dreamed of it. To see you again—even though all that is behind me—well, it's like magic. Of all the houses in the world, to be assigned this one."

He couldn't tell if that was a wink on her face, or a smirk, or merely a lip lifting in disbelief. You never can be sure with cats. Anyway, an eyebrow arched.

Pepper hissed at him, "What-the-Dickens, are you nuts? Are you a match without a sulfur head? Are you a cream soda about to get creamed? We don't talk to the enemy! We gotta get outta here! This whole place is gonna blow sky-high!" This wasn't strictly true but Pepper wasn't wasting any time being selective about her figures of speech. That's what panic can do. "Fat hairy girl's gonna pounce!"

McCavity swiveled her behind on the floor, centering herself for launch. Her whiskers trembled, marking the parameters of her peripheral vision, helping her to aim.

"What-the-Dickens! This ain't a suicide mission! Scat!" shouted Pepper again.

Gage, in his bed, turned. Even little tiny voices can wake up a sleeping human. He began to sit up in bed just as McCavity sprang.

What-the-Dickens was frozen, caught between what he had once believed and what Pepper was saying. He wanted to move, but he stood with arms opened wide. Even if McCavity was a murderess, how wonderful she looked, how dedicated, every whisker atremble with excitement, and her coppery eyes narrowing on him as if he were the one in the world she most desired.

Pepper dove and grabbed What-the-Dickens by his hair. She hoisted him two, three, six inches over the edge of the bed.

"You're insane!" she bellowed. "You're off your rocker." The cat's razor claws sank into the pillow behind where What-the-Dickens had stood, paralyzed with devotion.

The cat struck again. A sudden squall of duck down, released from the pillow, complicated her attack, and she missed What-the-Dickens. She caught Pepper, though—one sharp claw right through her wing—and brought her down under her paw.

Defeated, Pepper lost her hold of

What-the-Dickens, who dropped back on the rumpled bedclothes.

"No, no," said What-the-Dickens, coming to what was left of his senses.

"Hey," said Gage, rubbing his eyes, "you mad cat, what've you got there? Let it go."

Pepper screamed once or twice and she belted the cat square in the face with her coin purse. McCavity wasn't giving up, though. She hissed and snarled and snapped open her pink little mouth, a mouth well supplied with teeth designed to do serious damage.

What-the-Dickens scrambled back and forth. *What have I done? What should I do?*

He leaped onto the cat's head and sat down. Then he slid down her glossy forehead, stretching his legs to either side so as to drive her eyelids shut, blinding her.

Gage didn't notice What-the-Dickens. He was too busy grabbing at McCavity's forepaws. That cat nipped at him in rage, and not for the first time. The boy was brave, though. He didn't let go. He took McCavity's left paw in his hand and held it up in the air. Gravity did its work. Pepper's wing slipped off the claw without tearing further, like a loose blouse falling off a hanger.

Gage caught her before she collapsed underfoot on the floor.

"You dreadful cat, you've snagged a beautiful moth. Shame on you," said Gage. He grabbed the cat under her belly and hoisted her across the room. McCavity twisted, but Gage was bigger and stronger. What-the-Dickens had barely managed to leap aside off McCavity's face before Gage tossed the cat out into the hallway and closed the door on her.

What-the-Dickens ran under the dresser and watched from the gloom. His stomach heaved. That gray cat: that had been stark-white McCavity all along—McCavity, darkened by shadows.

"What *have* we got here?" said Gage, bringing Pepper back to his bed, and flipping on his bedside lamp.

Pepper blinked her eyes and tried to curl her wings over her head, imitating an autumn leaf in the act of drying out. But the damaged wing wouldn't curl, so she lay exposed in Gage's hand.

Terror, shame, pain, rage?

All of the above, maybe.

Hidden, forbidden, thought What-the-Dickens. *She must be mortified.*

"I don't believe my own eyes," said Gage. "McCavity has caught me a flying worm."

"I ain't a worm, you worm!" screamed Pepper, too terrified to play by the rules.

"A very skinny flying mouse?" Gage's voice was husky with disbelief, as if he thought he might be having some sort of psychotic episode.

"Let me go!"

"A very noisy, very skinny, sort of nasty, pint-size flying angel who speaks English?"

"Lemme *go,* you big ugly brute. You— ogre! You monster! You human being!"

"Oooh, got me there," said Gage. "Well, you've got my number. You've cracked my disguise. I *am* a human being. A kid. A boy. Now it's your turn. You look like a reject from the pages of some lady's book of simpery fairies of the garden. Are you the Spirit of Springtime or something?"

"If I give you some guesses and you can't guess, will you let me go?"

"Okay."

"Well, you've already guessed enough times: a worm, a mouse, an angel, and your bonus guess was a garden sprite of some disgusting sort. Wrong, wrongedy wrong. So let me go."

"Well, but you guessed *me* right," said Gage. "I'm a human. So I don't always keep my promises."

"Fiend," said Pepper, her face dropping. "Then everything they say about your kind is true."

"What do they say? And who says it?"

"That you're vicious, vain, and blind to the world. That you lie, cheat, and steal, and call it courtesy, cunning, and thrift. That you think cats like you. Hah! As if. And that you don't believe in wishes."

"Well, you're mostly right," said Gage. "Only we kids don't have too much chance to lie, cheat, or steal, and we try not to. I don't really know what adults do yet because I'm not an adult."

"I *am* right about humans," said Pepper, as much to herself as to her captor. "I seen more of them than you have. I'm, like, *totally* right."

What-the-Dickens thought, *Is she giving a message to me? Not to trust that boy whatever he says?*

"I believe in wishes, though," said Gage. "I mean, come on: I *would,* wouldn't I? I'm here having a debate with a cranky little exile

- 214 -

from some fairy tale? Talk about your alternative reality."

"You're having a dream," said Pepper in a suddenly sweet, dippy voice, as if she intended to lull Gage back to sleep. "A lovely dream. Ain't I lovely?" She flinched in a spasm of pain but tried to look lovely while flinching.

But he was having none of that.

"I used to have a dog, too," he said. "It was named Winnie-the-Poodle. McCavity chased her into the street and she got run over. Then I got three little parakeets called Orville and Wilbur and Charlotte. McCavity ate them all when I was at school. My parents said I can't get any more animals unless I get rid of the cat. But I can't get rid of her. You can't just disown a cat, even an evil cat you never liked."

What-the-Dickens dug his fingers into the splintery old oak of the dresser leg. To hear the word *evil* used to describe the creature he'd loved first and best . . .

"I take it back," said Pepper. What-the-Dickens could see she was trying every angle. "I'm impressed. Maybe you're a *kind* human. I didn't know they came in that variety. If you're so kind, will you let me go?"

"Not till you tell me who you are and where you came from," said Gage. "I just saved your life. You owe me."

Pepper couldn't give away the secrets of Northwest Sector, Division B—she couldn't. She looked resigned, and her spine curled a little as she folded her arms and shook her head. Then she closed her lips and pretended to lock them with an imaginary key, and throw the key over her left shoulder.

"Well, I have to go to the bathroom," said young Gage. "To keep you safe, I'm going to have to put you in here." He carried Pepper to a bamboo cage that sat on the top of a chest of drawers. "McCavity is sneaky. She can imitate a shadow very well. She can slip into the room at ankle-height when I'm just opening the door. That's how she got Orville and Wilbur and Charlotte, and I don't want her to get you. This is for your own protection, Sprite of the Night."

He opened the door and set Pepper in. She sank her teeth into the meat of his palm and tried to escape, but Gage closed the door and just rubbed his hand on his pajama top as if he'd gotten a mosquito bite.

"Don't worry," he told Pepper. "McCavity

can't open this latch, believe me. I've seen her try. Just stay well toward the middle of the birdcage floor in case she gets in somehow. She's got a long leg fitted with nasty claws. I'll be right back."

He left. Pepper and What-the-Dickens both watched the door like a hawk. The cat did not slink in — not this time.

What-the-Dickens flew up to the cage and threw his weight against the latch, but he wasn't strong enough to move it. He gasped, "What'll we do? Are you badly hurt? Can you fly?"

"Look," said Pepper, "this is a disaster. Total disaster. But I ain't gonna give the colony away. The rule drummed into us in nursery school is 'hidden and forbidden.' We remain hidden, but if we get caught, we are forbidden to squeal. Now Doctor Ill may have thrown me a coupla curve balls, but I'm not gonna sacrifice the whole compound just for revenge. Tempted though I might be. *You're* gonna have to do my final assignment, and then go back to the colony. Tell them I am missing and presumed croaked."

"What'll they do? Mount a rescue mission?" asked What-the-Dickens.

"No. I'll die in captivity very quickly. My body will shrivel up within a day. I'll look a whole lot like the dead leaf I was trying to imitate. By the end of the week, this boy-kid will begin to think he imagined the whole thing. But, What-the-Dickens! Are you listening?"

He was, but he was crying, too, and sniffling so loud he could hardly hear what Pepper was telling him.

"Listen *closely*. Nobody will care about this but me. Even so, it's what I want. This is my dying wish. Take this coin and finish the mission. Go to Lee Gangster's house and do the trade. Then rush back to the colony with both teeth: Gage's and Lee's. Complete my final mission in my name. Maybe they'll make me an Agent of Change posthumously."

"What does that mean?"

"I'll get my license even though I'm dead."

"What good is that kind of license?"

"Don't argue! He'll be back any second. Do you understand?"

"Pepper," said the orphan skibberee, "you forget I don't know how to navigate. My wings give me feelings. They give me impulses. They give me a bit of a lift, if you don't mind my saying so. But they don't give me any important *news* about anything. Just hints, suggestions, ideas. How am I going to carry out this mission without any instinct for it?"

"You're going to do it the old-fashioned way," said Pepper. "Pay attention, and I'll tell you what I know, and then, in more ways than one, you'll just have to wing it."

She described the very night-place in which this Tavenner house sat primly behind its fences, squarely on its lawns. What-the-Dickens tried to fasten the images in his head:

Draw back, draw higher into the sky. See the ground as a map beneath you. Tavenner house in the center: got it? Find a road to the south. Find a stand of beech trees on a knoll. Now draw higher, lean southwest, and center the beech trees in your mind. You'll see a slice of highway making a gentle curve at the southwest edge of the knoll. Follow the highway south to the next exit. Head east along the trunk road, second house on your right. If you hit the zoo, you've gone too far. A dingy white house with chimneys. Can't miss it. Got that?

What-the-Dickens repeated the instructions.

"Now, go," she said.

He hovered by the cage.

"What are you waiting for?" she said, hearing the sound of a toilet flushing in the room next door. "If, like most boys, he don't wash his hands, he's almost here again! Leave!"

"I want a kiss," he said.

"I'm not your girlfriend!" she screamed. "What, you want to kill me just a little bit faster?"

"I'm not your boyfriend," he answered. "I just want a kiss for luck. And to remember. This is my first kiss, you know."

She softened. "And it's my last," she replied. She kissed him through the bamboo bars: sweetly, quickly, memorably. "Now get outta here before you get caught. Take my pouch, it still has the coin we didn't give Gage. Use that for the trade."

"I thought skibbereen never stole teeth—"

"All the rules break when you're at the end," she replied. "At least I've just decided that. Now go, What-the-Dickens: please go. It will cheer me up in my last moments to think that you might have made it. But don't linger at the colony. Evacuate. They'll take action against you sooner or later. You're an alien, and they'll have no truck with aliens."

"What'll I do?" he said. "I mean, then? Without you?"

"Ask no questions," she said decisively, and closed her eyes. "Use your imagination. You'll make out all right."

He flew to the doorway and hovered above the lintel. When Gage returned, What-the-Dickens slipped out up high just as McCavity slipped in down low.

"Don't forget to floss!" cried Pepper madly, uttering the traditional farewell commonly used only by the old biddie skibbereen to their sewing society members.

❧ ❧ ❧

"Stop there," said Zeke. "Now I have to go to the bathroom."

When Zeke had left the room, Dinah said, "He's listening, you know."

"He's a brave, brave kid," said Gage. "Braver than I was at his age. You're lucky to have him as a brother. I admire him."

Since Dinah couldn't honestly reply, *And he admires you,* she changed the subject. "I think it is getting lighter. Don't you?"

"You're mixing up the story with the true night," said Gage. "That's the trouble with stories. It's still as dark as ever out there, Dinah. But morning will come. Very few things in the world are certain, but morning is one of them."

"It's always morning at some place in the world," said Dinah, looking out the window at the blackness. "Even when you're sad—when you're missing someone so much you can't say it—there's some place else in the world where the light is coming out again, as if for the first time."

"That's a bit soupy," said Gage, "though I'm not one to talk. You've been reading some of those books that Granny Menace despises so much?"

"We don't do a whole lot of reading except for Bible stories. But they're a lot about light coming in, too. Sort of."

Gage was chastened somewhat. "You're right about mornings. You know, in the middle of your own midnight swamp, there's always some other dawn story happening somewhere else that is just swell. Some baby being born to ecstatic parents, some unexpected happiness tripping up a tired commuter, some act of kindness interrupting a day of plodding. The notion that there are other good stories you'll never know is in itself kind of consoling. Don't you think?"

"That's the grown-up you talking now," said Dinah, as politely as she could. "I don't want that part, all the shiny meaning polished up all obvious and sound-bitey, just so I can get it. Save that for Zeke. Me, I just want to find out what happened to the two skibbereen."

She got up stiffly to use the bathroom when Zeke got back. "And to you," she added politely, "though I guess I know what happened to you, don't I?"

"So far," Gage said. He didn't seem offended.

⊷ EIGHTEEN ⊷

Perhaps What-the-Dickens was learning something. An hour had gone by since he and Pepper had landed at Gage Tavenner's house. Now the air had a different character; a thicker, more spoiled breath, as if the world waited till the most private part of the night to exhale its less flowery perfumes. Or maybe there was just a plumbing problem over at the zoo.

He recited the directions over and over again, scared he would forget them. His attention was interrupted though by his temper: he was angry at himself. *Why can't I interpret the amber twitches and vinegary sizzles I feel coursing up and down my wings? I can fly now, more or less, so I'm not beyond learning something new . . . but my instincts for communication with headquarters are missing. Or broken. Maybe a result of being born without a colony, without a clan, without a mother.*

I just can't interpret the lingo. I just don't get it.

He gained some height over the Tavenner house. As he rose, he felt a growing sense of distress at leaving Pepper behind. Every added yard of distance between them deepened the ache. Still, what could he do for her but fulfill her mission—their mission? This was his chance to prove his mettle, to show both the colony and Pepper that he was a capable skibberee even if born solo and, by the accident of his origins, a rogue.

The world below settled more or less into the map that Pepper had described. There was the road by the Tavenner house, grey in the cloud-blurred moonlight. And there, was that the knoll of beech trees? He climbed to a higher altitude and confirmed his position. Yes, for sure. To the south of the knoll ran the highway, and you couldn't mistake a highway for a river or a cart track, not with those red and white beads of light moving in coordination along it, northwest and southeast.

The headlights of trucks on overnight runs, or early-bird commuters? *Dawn will be here soon,* thought What-the-Dickens, *and there's so much to be done. Yes, indeed, and I see a lightening in the sky to the east. Not anything as obvious as orange or pink, just a softening of black-ness into a kind of charcoal. As if the night over there is hesitating.*

No time to lose. He had an idea—where had it come from? Ideas didn't come from central command, did they? Was it a scrap of memory about how the baby grisset, tumbling from the nest, had managed to save itself?

With the nerve that is born of panic, he folded his wings suddenly and plunged earth-ward. *The memory of Pepper will be all that is left of her in another twenty-four hours,* he thought. *I must do what I can to make sure the memory is heroic.*

So, Geronimo, and good-bye to all that, and here's looking at you, kid.

Toward the south-leading lane of the high-way he dove like a bungee jumper without a bungee. If his instincts were wrong, he would be dead sooner than Pepper—and there'd be no one left to carry on her memory, or to care about his. But it was worth the risk, to buy a little time, when time was so short.

Thirty feet above the pavement he flexed his wings to cup the air and slow his descent.

Readying, readying. If he dropped too quickly, he'd be smooshed on the fender of a truck like his cousin the moth. If he dropped too slowly, he'd miss his window of vacuum and end up drying in the morning sun, a tiny dot of skibberee moisture on the highway. . . .

An eighteen-wheeler threw up too much turbulence. A passenger car changed lanes too swiftly, too often. He had to find a mid-size vehicle, neither racing nor swerving, but holding its speed judiciously.

Here it comes. Ready, steady . . .

He angled out like a bomber coming in around a target, describing in the air a curve such as might be made by an ant spiraling downward on the outside of a plump teapot.

He positioned himself, always moving, always gauging, correcting, readying, steadying, and: now: *going.*

It worked! Worked it! It worked! Worked it! His thoughts tumbled over and over as he tumbled, too, in the slipstream of a midsize truck. Red, with black and gold letters on the two back doors.

GOODNESS BAKERY

THE BEST BAKED GOODS

And the exhaust smelled encouragingly

of raspberry jam coffee cake and cinnamon rolls.

The baker drove the Goodness Bakery delivery van at a brave sixty-two miles an hour (brave because the speed limit was fifty-five). The countryside blurred in a smear of black-and-light. In less time than it takes to tell, the truck passed a highway sign announcing the upcoming exit. What-the-Dickens kick-swam himself to the edge of the slipstream, and then jackknifed himself out of it, again tumbling over and over again in the stiller air.

He was lucky. He might have smacked into a milk house or a tractor shed, or the billboard screaming out

BUY IN NOW — THREE NEW HOUSING ESTATES!

BUILD TO YOUR CHOICE OF PLANS!

DAIRYLAND COMMON

GRANITE HEIGHTS

APPLETREE ACRES

But he survived.

It took him a minute for his memory to catch up with his body, but soon it did. He headed east along the trunk road, passed a schlumpy sort of house that had seen better days, and came to a second one that looked no better. But it did look familiar.

It was the house into whose chimney the rust-throated grisset had deposited him. The old fiend upstairs, heading for a hundred—*she* was Lee Gangster? Oh, the accident necessary to fiction! It was hard to believe, but he didn't have time to hang about in the air, gaping. To be alive at all was such a colossal coincidence that every other accidental luck paled by comparison.

There is work to be done. I'll do it. I'll manage. Coincidence arms me, but I do the work.

For Pepper, he told himself, and dove to the task.

What-the-Dickens remembered that the old lady liked to sleep with her window open, so access to the site was a cinch. There she was, sitting up in bed again, surrounded by volumes of poetry with poetic images printed on them: rows of daisies, bolts of lightning, streams of musical notes, parades of bugs, fences made out of bloody daggers, and a lot of books with appealing titles like *Oblivion* and *Morosity* and *The Collected Poems of Ella Wheeler Wilcox*.

"Is my family trying to tell me something?" she groused aloud, picking up a glass empty of all but the drowned remains of a segment of lime. She fished out the lime with gnarled fingers and sucked any remaining gin out of it. "I hardly think any of these are what you'd call a laugh riot. More like a farrago of gloom. Hardly restores my zest for living."

She opened up her mouth in a yawn. What-the-Dickens remembered she liked to grumble all night and then snore herself to sleep in the morning. But he couldn't wait for her to nod off. To save Pepper's reputation, he was going to have to break some rules.

He dusted off his wings, straightened his tunic, and took a deep breath. Before she had finished yawning, he flew before her and hovered a foot from her face. (This gave him a good look at her gums. She had only one natural tooth left; all the false teeth, in their serried ranks, were suspended in another glass of water, as before.)

"Is that tooth about to come out?" he demanded.

"Oh, it's you," she replied, hardly surprised. "Didn't I tell you I wasn't ready to die yet? I might not like the reading material in this waiting room, but that doesn't mean I want to see the Final Doctor."

"I'm not the Fairy of Death," he said patiently, "and I don't have time to explain. I want your tooth."

"This old thing?" She tapped it with a finger. "What, are you some kind of deranged tooth fairy with a fetish? Tooth fairies want milk teeth, buster; this is a gin prong. And I'm not surrendering it. At least one of my natural teeth is going to make it with me to one hundred, which is still a few months away. So buzz off, and take these books with you."

"I can't lift them," he said. "I'm only big enough to lift a tooth. I'll give you a quarter for it."

"I can't buy a new false tooth for a quarter."

"Give it to me." He ventured closer.

"Come any nearer and I'll trap you in the pages of posterity," she threatened. She picked up a tome and read from it. "'Up the airy mountain, / Down the rushy glen, / We daren't go a-hunting / For fear of little men.' That sounds like a good page on which to be interred, little man."

He tried again. "You read a lot, so you think you know everything. Well, guess what. I *am* the Fairy of Death, and I'm going to take your life from you if you don't give me your tooth."

She dabbed at her eyes with the edge of her sheet. "I talk a blue streak to keep myself amused, but that doesn't mean I'm ready to die," she said. "I'm just lonely, that's all. And now loneliness is playing tricks on me: I'm hallucinating a midget Angel of Death. Tell you what: Why don't you stay here and be my friend, and we can play tricks on the grandchildren downstairs? I'd be so much nicer if I had some company."

"Your tooth or your life," he repeated, trying to sound like a bully.

"You can have my false teeth," she offered grandly. "All of them. Go on. I mean it. I'll tell the insurance people that my grandson flushed them down the toilet. It'll take a month to get a new set, but what's a month? Another month of life, that's what, in all its joy and glory! Deal?"

What-the-Dickens paused. Tempting—had such riches ever been harvested by a single tooth fairy? Except for the space where Lee Gangster's real-life gin prong fit in, it was a complete set of uppers and lowers. Imagine the celebration! Imagine the gratitude of Doctor Ill! Maybe Silviana would add another Act to the Duty Pageant, honoring the triumph of What-the-Dickens. . . .

But it's the triumph of Pepper I'm committed to achieving, he remembered. Somewhat sadly, he said, "I can't close that deal. My job is in trades, but I'm not authorized—"

"Don't you have a superior you can speak to?" she interrupted. "Surely there's a Great Tooth Fairy in the sky or something who watches every little sparrow that falls senseless to the ground, and so on?"

"That's beyond my area of expertise," he said. "I'm taking the tooth. I'm sorry, Mrs. Gangster. It's my job." As he spoke, he removed his knapsack with the quarter in it.

Maybe I can spin around in the air like a top and build up speed and power. Then I might whack out the tooth while her mouth is open in astonishment at my prowess.

It might work. Riding the slipstream of the bakery truck had worked.

Lee Gangster's voice suddenly crumpled, and she sounded like the young girl she would have been nearly a century ago. "This is getting surreal. When you start imagining you're being molested in your own bed by the Tooth Fairy of Death, you've been hitting the sauce too much. Or reading too much fiction. Too much alone. Where's my mother? *She* always comes. Why doesn't she come? Mama!" she cried. "Mama!"

Perhaps the new note of anxiety in her voice carried farther than her usual carping, for though her volume had hardly risen, a door opened downstairs. Feet pattered in the hallway. "Grandma?" said a voice. "Are you all right?"

"Who's there?" called Lee Gangster. "Who's that?"

What-the-Dickens paused. He couldn't smack an old woman in the face who was calling for her mother. He just couldn't. *Sorry, Pepper,* he thought. He lowered the satchel.

The door opened. What-the-Dickens had the presence of mind to spring to an ornately carved frame hanging on the wall. It surrounded a portrait of an early Gangster, now presumably deceased, though possessed of a magnificent overbite that any red-blooded skibberee would drool over.

"What's the matter, Grandma?" asked the grandchild, a small boy in cowboy pajamas.

A small boy with a worried expression—a furrowed brow, an uneven buzz cut, dirty fingernails—and a gap in his dental lineup where his left front tooth should be.

"I've had an interview with the Angel of Death," she gabbled, "and the visitor is still around here somewhere! Listen, Lee darling, do this for Granny. Find the cunning little creature and kill him for me, will you?"

"Grandma," said her grandson patiently, "you've had a bad dream. . . ."

What-the-Dickens didn't stay to hear the rest. He fled out the open door and spiraled down the stairs. He was looking for the bedroom of the grandson—the *other* Lee Gangster. He knew he would find the appropriate tooth there, and the pillow under which he could leave the skibberee's calling card—the coin of the realm.

❧ NINETEEN ❧

Pepper quivered, like a drying seedpod rasping along the dirt in a stiff wind.

She had not experienced dying before, so she was curious. But she also hadn't experienced such hearty emotion before, or not so she'd recognized at the time. True, she'd felt for the colony a distant sort of patriotism that had been romance and religion alike to her. Beyond this, she'd had ambitions—ambitions to a private name and a license to work abroad at night. But that was about it. She hadn't had *feelings.* Heavens. They weighed so much—

—they weighed so much—

—she could hardly flap her wings to get her blood going and dispense those pesky feelings.

Nor can I name them, she thought. *I got neither the skill nor the practice.*

With some effort she turned her head to look at her captor. He was a human, and humans were known to be stuffed with feelings. It was their curse and their charm. How did he manage it?

Having grown up in a skibbereen colony, Pepper knew more about human beings than What-the-Dickens could. She knew enough to be scared out of her wits. She understood that humans could be vicious, stupid, corrupt, and insensitive.

They could lie with a talent that beggared belief.

Frequently they smelled awful, too.

In the plus column—as if she could ever add one and one!—Pepper conceded that Gage was only a child. And human children haven't yet had time enough to grow crooked. Human children are often breezy of spirit, warm of heart, devout in their prayers, and hopeful to boot. They like stories, they run and shriek and kick balls across the grass for no apparent reason. They only occasionally stink, for nothing in them has begun to decay.

And this lad Gage, her client, seemed decent enough.

Except for the little business of his locking her in a cage until she died. That was in the minus column, and it was a big fat minus.

The boy had drawn up a chair to his desk. Perched there, he lowered his chin onto his folded hands on the desktop, so he could look through the narrow bamboo struts of the cage and watch Pepper in captivity.

"Are you comfortable?" he asked.

Skibbereen aren't supposed to talk to their humans. Skibbereen in captivity are supposed to pretend to be bugs and pass away as briskly as possible.

But I feel—disobedient, thought Pepper. *Worried enough to feel—is it called—chatty?*

"You just don't look comfortable," he said. "What if I folded up a washcloth and set it inside for a kind of little mattress? If we had marshmallows in the house I could creep downstairs and get one for your pillow. It'd be just perfect."

He looked sad at the thought that he lived in a house lacking in marshmallows.

I'll resist the urge to talk to him. I'll force myself to sit up and fold my legs and swivel around so my back is to him.

Though the labor of the gesture exhausted her, she managed. She felt no pride in her stubbornness, but she liked noticing her feelings. You *could* keep changing, even on your deathbed.

"Don't be like that!" he said. "I'm just trying to keep you safe. You should have seen what McCavity did to Charlotte, Orville, and Wilbur. It was disgusting. Feathers and blood everywhere."

"Why don't you get rid of her?" she snapped over her shoulder; suddenly she couldn't help herself. "What kind of a person harbors a known murderess like that?"

"Who would want her? Who could put up with her?" he replied. "I can't send McCavity to the cat pound. They might put her down—kill her—and then I'd be just as guilty as she is."

"You'll be as guilty as she is if you don't let me go."

"Oh, are you worried? Don't worry. I like you, you know. I'll take care of you. You can be my pet. Nothing good ever happened to me before this."

"Enjoy it while it lasts," she said aloud, before she could stop herself. *I'll die before you can show me off to your friends, kid. I'll be a browning leaf stem, no more than that.*

It was almost as if he could read her mind. "I won't give you away to anyone. I don't have any friends anyway. I can just enjoy it being the two of us. But now I know: I'm a person that something can happen to. I never guessed. I always thought I was going to be the kind of person nothing ever happened to. I'd have to stand in the background of all the class photos, being blurred to everyone, and blurred to myself."

It sounded familiar: like being a skibberee who failed at her exams and had her license suspended. "You don't get out enough," she said.

"I'm a child: what are my options?" he replied.

"I ain't here to do career counseling for a ten-year-old," she snapped, and added to herself, *I'm trying to collect my thoughts before I die.* "Why don't you go, oh, play a board game?"

"Board games are boring. After the first time, you know how they have to end. It's only a question of how you get there."

"Then read a book. Books can end any number of ways."

"I don't have any books. We can't afford them. We're not what you'd call prosperous."

"That's what libraries are for."

"The community library is only open on Saturday mornings, and on Saturdays we always go to tailgate fairs and sell my mom's pot holders and my dad's hand-painted wooden duck decoys."

Pepper gave up. She began to shudder with an unfamiliar chill.

"Are you cold?" said Gage. "Can I get you a blanket of some sort? I have a little pencil case with a sliding door. I could line it with tufts of cotton pulled off the ends of ear swabs. You could stretch out in it."

"That sounds like a coffin. That's human practice. No thanks." But Pepper was oddly pleased at the attention.

"What if I bring the desk light closer to warm you up?" he said, and pulled the gooseneck of his lamp over the cage.

She shrieked. What was he trying to do, bake her dry as a skeleton?

Gage swung the lamp back. "Well, are you hungry, then?" he asked.

"For freedom, for flight, for privacy," she replied, "Yes. For food, forget it."

"Am I supposed to let you go?" he said. "Is it that sort of a thing? Don't you have to give me a wish then, for my charity?"

"I don't got to give you anything," said her words, but she felt her eyes steam up, in anger or confusion. Couldn't this human being do a kind thing without being paid? True, tooth fairies were in the business of trade, but weren't humans rumored to be capable of kindness? Sometimes?

"Come on, let's be fair. I saved your life. McCavity would've torn you to shreds. If you don't give me a wish, can't you give me *something* I don't have? Why don't you tell me about yourself?"

"I'm hardly here anymore. I don't count."

"I know so little about anything," he said, "but you count to me."

If I start thinking about counting, I'll confuse myself. "You don't read enough," she said. "That's how to learn something about something."

"We covered that already. Tell me a story about yourself."

"Once upon a time," she said, "there was a little tiny fairy named Bluebell Berrybush. Every day she flitted from flower to flower minding her own business. One day she was trapped by a grotesque child, and she died a hideous miserable death, but still minding her own business, which was a comfort to her in her final moments. The end."

"Your name is not Bluebell Berrybush," he said. "I may be only ten, but give me a break. I'm not a nincompoop."

"What's the least amount I can tell you before you grant my freedom?" she asked. "I don't got long, you know."

"I'm not sure," he said. His eyes looked large, as if he were surprised that his gambit showed signs of paying off. "Start, and keep on, and we'll know when you get there."

"You drive a hard bargain," she said, but the sparkles in her wings were beginning to fade, and her toes curled downward a little.

"You got my tooth," he said. "Are you really the Tooth Fairy?"

She hid her face in her hands. "You could say so."

"I thought there wasn't any such thing as the Tooth Fairy. That's what all the big kids say."

"Big kids know everything, don't they." She was surprised she had the strength to sound sarcastic. "Does that prove I don't exist, just because big kids grow out of believing in me?"

Gage wasn't a quick thinker. He couldn't answer the question. "The Tooth Fairy. Wow!" he said. "There really is one. I didn't think those old stories and legends had any truth to them. Can you shed any light on Santa Claus?"

"Not my department."

"Easter Bunny? Four-leaf clovers? Leprechauns and rainbows and pots of gold?"

"Pots of bunk if you ask me, but I'm not an expert witness."

"Wishing on a star? Wishing on a coin thrown in a fountain?"

Pepper didn't want to talk about wishes, because a wish was just exactly what she wished to have the use of right now. She drew her arms around her small legs and huddled into a tighter bundle. "No comment."

Gage could tell the subject of wishing was a hot one. "If you won't give me a wish," he said in a low voice, "maybe I could give you one. What do you wish for now?"

"You know perfectly well. I'd rather die as a free agent than as a captive."

"But you'd die alone," he replied. "I know what it's like to be alone myself—I'm an only child. It's no good."

Pepper hesitated.

Then she broke another rule.

"I wouldn't die alone," she whispered. "I'm not the only one. There are others of us."

"No!" he whispered back.

"Yes," she said, "but if I tell you all about it, I'll jeopardize their safety. We live by—what was that nursery motto they hammered into us?—'camouflage and subterfuge.' The most basic rule is not to draw attention to ourselves. Still, I give it to you straight: Let me go, and I try to make it to the colony. At least I'll die within sight of my home."

"You're nearby? Here in Fern Hill?" He was almost breathless with excitement. "Right near here?"

"Use your head. How else could we do our work unless we had local chapters?" she said.

"Can I see it? Can I take you there?"

"Huh. I can just imagine the things those jokesters would say if I brought a human boy home for breakfast."

"But—if it's near enough for you to reach by flying, surely I could walk there. . . ."

Her hunger for home—as strict and uncompromising as her home was—raked through her. She convulsed with longing, her chin touching her toes. "Don't tempt me," she begged. "We're supposed to die alone, and if you talk to me about returning home, I don't know what I'll do."

"Let me help," he said. "I didn't ask for you to come here. I didn't set McCavity on you. All I ever wanted was some news of the outside world—the world outside this safe, safe, safe house. You've given me some news. Come on. Why not? I won't have to get too near. I won't make you introduce me to anyone. I can set you down somewhere nearby, and then just stand back and watch."

And blow our cover for all time, thought Pepper. *We'd have to abandon the colony by tomorrow night. We'd move out the bank, we'd hire woodworms and carpenter ants to chew our careful chambers into disrepair so thorough it could never be read as a built environment. The Undertree*

*Common would be history, and who knows what
the future would hold for Division B of the Northwest Sector?*

*But who knows what the future holds for me,
either, except death if I say no,* she thought trem-
blingly, with a rare, if desperate, courage.
Courage, or dread. Or both.

❧ ❧ ❧

"Holding a tooth fairy hostage — how could you
do such a thing?" Dinah demanded to know this at
once. "That doesn't sound like you at all, Gage."

"I was lonely. And bored. It's hard to explain.
And my parents were strict."

"Why didn't you surf the web?"

"Dinah. I don't know how to break this to
you —"

"Oh, right. I remember. You were in the rural
backwater. The dark ages of dairyland. And your
family wasn't rich. You didn't rely on the Internet
and iPods and cell phones."

Of course, I don't have those things either, Dinah
thought. *Though what good would it do me now if
I did?*

She sat in the new dark ages and thought
about that.

❧ TWENTY ❧

What-the-Dickens felt the dawn nearing. He sensed it by instinct, not by prior experience.

Something was coming of instinct, then. Maybe something more. He listened carefully.

Bugs. Grasses curling earthward with a billion papery sounds, as the ritual of condensation set small but heavy beads of moisture on every available blade. Things dripping from trees. Animals in burrows retiring their dreams till tomorrow night, if another tomorrow night would come for them. Other animals, the nocturnal brigade, waddling home, slithering home, sluicing home through the currents of freshening air.

The world belongs to the animals, thought What-the-Dickens, *and no one knows it, not even them.*

Other skibbereen, braver than What-the-Dickens, might have turned back to attempt a daredevil rescue of Pepper. But dawn was nearly here, and the orphan skibberee had no time to worry over his choice. He would keep his word to Pepper. He would deliver the tooth he had collected from young Lee

Gangster. Toward Undertree Common he headed, as directly as his navigational instincts could lead him.

Instinct might be good for some things, but not for everything. What-the-Dickens flew for a few precious moments before realizing that he had headed in the wrong direction. He'd started toward the highway, and that was the direction—northwest—back toward the fussy antiseptic house of the Tavenners, where Pepper was caged. So he veered to go the other way, counterclockwise, over the zoo and up toward Undertree Common from the opposite direction. Completing a circular route.

Passing within range of the zoo—so near he could hear the rumble of elephant stomachs anticipating breakfast—What-the-Dickens had his brainstorm. Though he couldn't rescue Pepper, he could do more than secure her reputation.

He could make her a legend.

It would mean lying. But he was a rogue and a rebel, so what did he care?

He swept down toward the zoo. *Free the tooth! Free the tooth!* Hah, he'd had *some* instinct he was a tooth fairy from early on, hadn't he?

Free the tooth was just what he'd done, first time out, without a single nursery lesson about it.

I'll reclaim that tiger tooth I hid there, if it hasn't been cleared away. When I get back—just before dawn, if my timing allows it—I'll present Old Flossie and Doctor Ill with the tooth of Gage Tavenner, and the tooth of the young Lee Gangster, and then I'll toss on the table my big kahuna, my winner-take-all bauble. I'll say nonchalantly, "Oh, yes, and Pepper picked up this in her spare time, and sent it on as a memento. You can't identify it? Tiger tooth. Come nearer—it won't bite. Ha, ha! Plant this baby and see what comes up. Maybe not your garden-variety wishing candle. Maybe a wishing torch."

He found the stand that sold cotton candy, ice creams, popcorn, soda pop, and beer. There was the tooth, right where he'd left it, just inside a mousehole where a respectable clan of mice huddled. (Could they be distant relatives of Muzzlemutt?)

They scurried over one another and rubbed their paws, fretting. How much it must have cost them, to guard this gargantuan tooth. He nodded at them as he grabbed hold of it but he didn't bother to speak aloud. The languages of animals were kept secret from human and skibbereen alike. The silliness of him, trying to talk to McCavity. How young he'd been when he was first born. Dreadful, really.

But what a tooth this was. Still powerfully rank, notched as if by an awl, a monolith of dead bone designed to rend flesh from flesh.

Now that he knew skibbereen weren't programmed to approach animals for their teeth, What-the-Dickens had the sense to be terrified of his earlier bravado with the tiger. He almost retched with the memory. What *had* he been thinking about?

Not much—clearly. He'd been looking for McCavity and he'd gotten distracted by an apparition.

He was going to have to fly more slowly this final leg, for the tiger tooth wouldn't fit in his change pouch. He'd have to clutch it to his chest with his hands. So he wasn't even able to wave at the family of mice who followed him to the door of the mousehole.

He launched awkwardly, bumblingly. He was halfway over the tiger house when something peculiar happened.

The intermittent spritzing and fritzing of his wings—the instructions from headquarters that he'd never been able to interpret, and so he'd learned to ignore—began to bite at him, from inside. It was as if the carbonated sizzle suddenly took on a meaning. It began to ebb and course with a pattern.

Complete with punctuations—pauses—periods. Only this wasn't a written language, and it wasn't messages from Central. *Come here,* it said. *Come here.*

"I'll be late," he said aloud. The mice below, more or less waiting to see him disappear, seemed to wave.

Come here, said the message in his wings. *I want to see you.*

"I haven't come this far to be distracted now," he said. "I mean, can't this wait?"

COME HERE!

"Okay, okay," he said, though he didn't know to whom he spoke.

He dove in, following the call by assessing the strength of the impulses in his wings. The call took him through a window with iron slats in it. There, wise as wilderness and fierce as fire, sprawled the Bengal tiger known as Maharajah.

The tiger asked, *Did you take my tooth out?*

"Yes," said What-the-Dickens. "Do you need it back?"

No, said Maharajah. *I just wanted to know.*

"Oh," said the skibberee. "Well, you're welcome. You don't want to eat me or anything?"

You can go, now that I've said my part.

"But how can I understand you?" said What-the-Dickens. "Animals can't talk, and I can't talk animal."

I don't bother myself with questions like that, said Maharajah. He sniffed the air as if detecting the aroma of zookeeper making her predawn rounds with buckets of raw meat for breakfast.

I will say, continued the tiger, *I am not talking, strictly speaking. I am growling rather low in the back of my throat. If you're able to interpret the growl, that's your talent at language, not mine.*

"Oh, my," said What-the-Dickens, and he realized the tiger was telling the truth. It was the pulses in his wings that were forming into impressions of thoughts, structures of meaning. The tiger hadn't even opened his mouth.

One thing more, said the tiger.

"Yes?"

If I taught you one more thing, that would make—?

"Two?" said What-the-Dickens. "Two things?"

Exactly.

"Enjoy your breakfast," said What-the-Dickens. "I gotta fly."

And fly he did.

As he lifted up, he found himself wondering, *Did I hear something no one else can hear? Or did I imagine it? Did that really happen? Did Maharajah summon me? And did I obey? Is it a talent at language, like he said? Was it a vision?*

You never can *be sure with cats, can you?*

Who would ever believe me if I tell them I've talked to a tiger?

And what task or privilege does that put on me, if I did?

Now the eastern sky was less like grey and more like glass—colorless, ready to take an impression. Had there been clouds in the sky, they would have been stained with coral and gold. As it was, the last few stars winked out in the west as the horizon began to steam with the advent of the sun. In a little while, a stain of light would break over the hills. Then that first lancing beam of day would pin into place for all time the reputation of Pepper: as a loser, or as a qualified Agent of Change in absentia (absent due to her untimely death), or—what What-the-Dickens most devoutly hoped—as a tiger in her own right, worth memorializing in her own pageant. . . .

His reflections were torn in shreds by the sound of wind through talons. Talons? Yes, the claws, strong as bronze, of an old owl on his way home after a night of hurly-burly, and hungry as an owl can be even with the greasy remains of a small vole still smeared in his beak.

But we skibbereen aren't terribly appealing to predators, thought What-the-Dickens, madly trying to fly faster. *Are we?*

Maybe not; but there was a little hint of tiger still lingering on the tiger tooth, and an owl is a carnivore. . . .

Help! shrieked What-the-Dickens—not with his mouth, for his head was down and his lips closed, every ouncelet of him trying to imitate a bullet. *Help. Help.*

Maharajah, royal creature: Break the bars of your cage and leap to help me, as I helped you. . . . I know you can hear me. I believe it. I believe it.

The owl bore down. What-the-Dickens could hear the wind slicking through the owl's wings, but the air remained calm. An owl attacks without turbulence.

Help, he thought again, the kind of thought you have when there is no other thought left to have. *Help, please. Help.*

Help came, swifting in from the right, a crazed blob of lopsided traveler, weaving and bobbing, then intercepting the owl, and plucking What-the-Dickens out of harm's way.

The rust-throated grisset, bumpy in her navigation as usual, lurched down to the west, and the owl was too big to bank swiftly enough to follow. *What're you doing here, you wonderful accident?* said What-the-Dickens.

She answered him, in her way, which wasn't exactly loquacious, but cheery enough, and welcome in any case. *Flap flap,* she said, *flap flap! Home and back, home and back. Where is home? There is home. Are you my baby? I like to keep in touch. Blood's blood, and kith is kin.*

He didn't know if these were words, or thoughts, or just sympathies without words. He couldn't yet tell. Maybe he'd never know.

He knew what to answer, though. She was as close as he'd ever come to having a mother, even if she had once tried to feed him to her other children. *Yes, I'm your baby,* he said, which seemed to make her happy, though it didn't make her fly any more directly. She lurched like a kite at the mercy of opposing winds.

The cloverleaf appeared below them as the owl circled and then decided to go home and nurse his grievances and digest that vole.

What-the-Dickens knew that if he told the rust-throated grisset to drop at once toward the arrival stump, she would mean well but probably veer astray. This was how grissets survived predators themselves, flying so unpredictably that even they didn't know where they were headed.

So, apologetically, What-the-Dickens did a rude and graceless thing. He wrenched himself around in the clutch of the rust-throated grisset, and he opened his little mouth, and he bit her in the thigh.

Ingrate, barked the grisset, and flinched. Her grip relaxed. What-the-Dickens fell toward the ground, racing on a bull's-eye course, and the sun readied its hems of light in preparation for its grand entrance.

Keep in touch, fluted the grisset, family-minded and a mother at heart, even when her stepchildren bit her in the thigh. *Don't be a stranger, stranger! Just call out my name and, you know, I might not hear you, but I'll try!*

Maybe she said that. Or maybe it was just her usual off-key commentary about the skittish nature of happenstance.

The skibberee kept his arms around the tiger tooth. The satchel with the Gangster tooth and the Tavenner tooth bounced painfully against his spine. Soon he was close enough to see Old Flossie and the skibbereen beginning to duck for cover in case he hit the runway full-force and splattered himself in a six-foot wave of skibberee guts.

He remembered his maneuvers in entering the slipstream of the bakery delivery truck on the highway. Now he revised them for a full-gravity encounter. He arched his wings into two canopies, imitating a parasail, or a pair of hinged maple seeds. He slowed himself down so suddenly that he dropped the tiger tooth.

Like a missile, it fell to the stump and drove in, point first, a kind of landing stump on a landing stump.

There his feet settled, as graceful as tumbling lima beans could do.

The skibbereen raised their foreheads above the floor of the trunk and peered, wide-eyed, from their places of safety. They all saw What-the-Dickens lower his wings and fold them against his back. Only then did the sun strike him straight in the face, making the point that no one present could deny. He had gotten in on time. Not a moment to spare, but on time nonetheless.

DAWN

THE NOISE WOKE UP REBECCA RUTH, but not Zeke, not at first. He rolled over and snored on. Dinah, her whole mind filled with a world of tigers and owls, grissets and skibbereen, kids and teeth and Goodness bakers, couldn't shift her focus fast enough. Not until Gage had leaped to his feet and crashed into the wall, and sworn a most un-Ormsby-like curse, did she realize what it was.

Gage was lunging for the telephone. The phone was ringing.

He garbled into the receiver, "The phone's working—it's working!" as if the person phoning couldn't have guessed.

Dinah grabbed Rebecca Ruth to shush her morning lamb-like bleat, which could become a tiger roar in about three seconds. "Who's my baby pet?" crooned Dinah, rocking Rebecca Ruth with too much vigor.

"Hello," she heard Gage say. "Bad connection—speak up! Is this you?"

His tone more normal, he continued, "Tavenner here." He scratched his head, rucking up his hair. "Yes, she's back; she didn't stay out long. We're all here and we're fine."

Oh. Must be one of those deputies. Oh, well.

Still, the phone was working now; that was something. Dinah wished she could hear both parts of the conversation.

"What's the news?" asked Gage. "Did you have any luck at getting the temporary wall up? Any chance of power today?"

Dinah could hear a metallic sort of harangue filtering through the earpiece.

"Look," answered Gage. "Didn't I explain this last night? Mrs. Ormsby was having a medical emergency. Her stock of insulin was spoiled when the first power failure canceled the refrigeration, and their generator wouldn't kick on. I would have made the effort to drive her over the ridge road myself—"

The sound, quite possibly, of a *damn* from the other end of the line.

"—but I wasn't trained to help her in case we

couldn't get to proper attention, and her husband knows more than I do about her condition. And of course they didn't dare take the children with them, knowing what was being said about the ridge road. Is it passable now?"

Dinah watched his face. How did adults manage to support faces made out of concrete? Showing nothing?

"Well, we're all fine," he said. "You can report in that you've heard—"

After another few seconds, listening to blather, Gage turned and crooked his finger at Dinah. "They want to hear your voice to make sure I'm telling the truth," he said. "They've gone insane with stress and fatigue. They think I'm an ax murderer or worse, taking advantage of my younger cousins."

Dinah wrenched the phone from Gage. "I'm here—I'm fine," she barked. "Gage is doing fine."

"What's he doing?" It was that lady deputy. Rosa Herrera.

"Telling stories."

"Hmmm. Okay, girl. You all take care. If we can get back that way today, we'll pick up anyone ready and waiting. We'll leave behind anyone who has decided to play hide-and-seek on us. You got me on that one, honey? *Stay put.* And I'm not above smacking your butt if I catch you at any funny business. But it won't be before noon, earliest. Best case scenario, the lower road will be passable. *If* they can get the transformer fixed, and *if* the South River drawbridge is still there and functioning. Here's hoping." Even as Deputy Rosa Herrera was hanging up the phone, Dinah could hear that the woman's attention was moving on: she was barking at someone else, "Now, about those preemies at the Mountainside clinic . . ."

The line went dead. There was still a dial tone, for now. But there was no one useful to call. No way to find out what had happened to them.

Dinah hung up the receiver. "No one really knows where they are," she said to Zeke, who was rubbing his eyes and sitting up now. "If they made it over the ridge road, everything might be okay. But it still could be a while before they can get back to us."

"If they made it," said Zeke. "If they could find someone with a fresh supply of insulin. Properly refrigerated. If and if. We *ought* to spend a little time in prayer."

"First things first," said Gage, "and the first thing is that someone needs a diaper change."

"There are no more diapers," said Dinah.

"Paper towels and packing tape," said Gage. "Who says English teachers are useless in a crisis?"

"Brekkie," said Rebecca Ruth. "Brekkie brekkie now."

"Guess what we have for breakfast!" said Dinah cheerily. "Water!"

The kids ate water and tuna fish and peaches and baby carrots. They saved the candy bars. Then, since it was not yet dawn—not on a cloudy night of storm—Dinah lugged Rebecca Ruth back into the front room, and they settled in a twitchy heap, waiting for the light to arrive, what light there might be.

Gage had two aspirin for breakfast, and water. "Ahh," he said. "A balanced diet: one aspirin for each hand."

Zeke went to the bathroom and was in there longer than usual. *Maybe he's crying,* Dinah thought. *He shouldn't let the faucet run for an hour.*

Zeke could be a bully about prayer sometimes. Dinah didn't want to have to argue with him. "Get started on the story again," she told Gage. "Before he gets back."

"Give me a break. You're merciless." Gage rubbed his eyes with the heels of his hands. "Let me come up to room temperature, will you?"

Dinah didn't plan to say what she said next; it just came out. "You were asleep, and you jumped so fast for the phone. You were hoping that phone was for you," she observed. "You want someone to care about what's happening to you, too—not just to us. Don't you."

You have *someone of your own,* she thought.

"I'm doing just fine," he said, "for a sleep-deprived citizen of our fair land." He scratched his scalp and grinned. "*None of your business.* But I'll say this, sweetheart: To feel all alone sometimes doesn't mean you're going to feel alone forever."

"Tell me about it," she replied. Her voice sounded cold.

"I will," he promised. "Do you remember what happened last?"

"What-the-Dickens made it back safely," said Dinah. Then without warning her own eyes ridiculously filled up, stinging hot. "He made it. He made it. He made it."

❧ TWENTY-ONE ❧

"*You* again!" said the stump mistress. "You're the burdock stuck to my behind, aren't you? *You're* not expected back. Didn't you get the message?"

"There's been an emergency," said What-the-Dickens. "I have to report a catastrophe."

"Whatever," said Old Flossie. She sounded as if What-the-Dickens could say nothing that might deserve her full attention. Indeed, she turned to address the runway assistants. "Speaking technically, the arriving agent needs to touch down *on the runway* by exactly the first ray of sunlight. But this wastrel is standing on some sort of plinth, not on the runway itself. Make a note of it."

"It's not a plinth," said What-the-Dickens. "It's a tooth, a tiger tooth. Now, about Pepper—"

"About Pepper," said Old Flossie, "—or the skibberee previously known as Pepper—I note that she is absent. She hasn't fulfilled her mission. She'll be dealt with accordingly. Pity, but there you are." She put her hand to her eyes and scanned the skies. "Even she can't argue that she *almost* made it. Where is she?"

"Steady yourselves for bad news," said What-the-Dickens feelingly. "She's been hurt, and captured."

He expected this report to be greeted with silence, at least. But Old Flossie only harrumphed and remarked, "She's been well-trained. She'll know what to do." The other skibbereen, giggling without much focus, returned to their tasks.

They picked up little whisks made of five

or six evergreen needles and swept the tree stump clean. Then, in artful artlessness, the welcoming crew arranged several dead leaves and a pinecone on it. *Very convincing,* thought What-the-Dickens. Any human being tramping through the woods would imagine that nothing was amiss. Nature was busy rotting and thrusting itself into life again with its usual force, incoherence, and charm.

Without comment What-the-Dickens surrendered the Tavenner tooth and the Gangster tooth. The tiger tooth he would not surrender. "I shall deliver it personally to Doctor Ill," he said. "A token in memory of Pepper."

"In memory of whom, dear?" asked Old Flossie pointedly. "Anyway, I don't believe you're welcome here."

He followed her into the sweet haven of Undertree Common anyway. The various domestic skibbereen were at work, keeping the colony clean and orderly. Each at the assigned task. Unnamed, uncounted, and untroubled.

Then, suddenly, there was Silviana, the very same, in her full skirts sweeping along a corridor reciting something to herself.

What-the-Dickens felt respect and nerve bloom in him at once, and before he could talk himself out of it, he reached out and touched her on the shoulder as they drew abreast of each other.

"You were wonderful at the Duty Pageant," he told her.

She reeled back against the wall, far more startled than he'd expected her to be. "Heavens!" she said.

"I'm sure everyone says this to you all the time but—well, I'm new—and I never saw anything like it before."

"I have no doubt," she said, regaining her composure. And fluttering her eyelids.

"And I have some terrific new material for you—about Pepper and a tiger tooth. It'll wow 'em."

"You don't talk to the likes of her, you," said Old Flossie, and tried to give him the back of her hand, but he ducked.

"My name is Silviana," she said. "I *have* a name," she asserted, and curtsied, mostly to herself.

"Deeply impressed," said What-the-Dickens. "I do too. What-the-Dickens, at your service."

"If you've decided to oppose Doctor Ill, let's get it over with," said Old Flossie, tugging at What-the-Dickens. "We mustn't keep Doctor Ill waiting."

"I haven't decided to oppose anyone," said What-the-Dickens. "I want to explain to him about Pepper. Maybe he'll have some idea about what to do."

"I have no doubt," said Silviana, more insistently than before.

"Miss Silviana, you must forgive him, and forget all about this," said the stump mistress. "He's a simpleton, no more, no less, and he won't be in residence much longer."

"I have no doubt about *that*," she replied, a bit wistfully, and she fled down the hall in a thistly rustle of skirts.

"She has no doubts," mused What-the-Dickens. "None at all. I have nothing *but* doubts."

"A skibberee who doesn't know when to clam up is a skibberee with a big problem," barked Old Flossie. "Now, not another word out of you until Doctor Ill asks you a question."

They walked on. *I'm more at home here now,* thought What-the-Dickens, *because I know it better. I know this corridor, these lights, this stump mistress.*

But I'm less at home here now, too. Because I know it better.

The paradox made his wings ache.

"He's cruel, isn't he?" said What-the-Dickens. "The crown, I mean. Your boss."

"Ask no questions!" said Old Flossie sternly, and at once, as if she'd anticipated the remark. "He has our good at heart. It's easy to prattle off an opinion about his manner or methods, but he's kept us safe for many years. In the world at large, we're small." She continued in a softer voice. "You're very young yet, and preposterously thick. Perhaps you haven't quite taken in the measure of us. We're *quite* small. Very, very small and fragile. He's our crown. Don't disrespect him."

"That mouse he's muzzled. And rides around on!" Suddenly What-the-Dickens was offended. "Hardly better than caging a Bengal tiger."

"He lost the use of his legs, you know. You, the nosy question-asker, haven't asked how."

"Pepper called it a dental accident."

"Everything in our lives is a dental

accident, you idiot. Actually, the incident was an attack by the little vermin who call themselves the colony of Sequoia Heights. Northwest Sector, Division D. Uppity sort. Doctor Ill was the first one into the fray, you know. The crown of Sequoia Heights was riding a captive iguana, who savaged Doctor Ill's legs. But Doctor Ill never paused. He's a military hero. Bolstered by his courage, our troops withstood the attack, and we fended off our enemies. He wasn't Doctor Ill back then. He was a mere Agent of Change. Name of Aking."

What-the-Dickens raised an eyebrow. So an Agent of Change *could* become an upper? In certain circumstances? Pepper hadn't known this.

Old Flossie misunderstood his silence. "The name Aking derives from 'baking soda.'"

"Oh."

"So he knows strategy firsthand," finished Old Flossie. "Now shhhh, we're here." They knocked and were bade to enter the crown's chamber.

Muzzlemutt prowled back and forth in his little cage. Doctor Ill was reading an old scrap of advertising copy about mintyfresh dentifrice.

"Oh, it's the little anomaly, what's-its-name," said Doctor Ill, with boisterous good humor.

"What-the-Dickens," he said.

"Yes, that's it. And your accomplice, that quirky good-for-a-joke agent-in-training. What was her name?"

"Pepper," he answered, a little irritably. "Don't you remember? She was on a mission last night—a final mission to qualify for her license as an Agent of Change."

"Of course," said Doctor Ill blandly. What-the-Dickens had the sense that Doctor Ill would have said "Of course" in response to any report he heard, whether it be that Pepper the tooth fairy had come home triumphantly, or had been reported missing in action, or by popular acclaim had been nominated as the next President of the United States.

"I have something distressing to report," began What-the-Dickens, but Old Flossie nudged him and hissed in his ear, "Are you incapable of remembering the rules? You don't speak until you are asked a question."

"What's the report, stump mistress?" asked Doctor Ill.

"Most of the agents returned with their *matériel*. The rogue element here, What-the-Dickens, arrived more or less on time, having secured the teeth of both clients." Old Flossie sounded impressed despite herself. "The rookie on probation is late and presumed incompetent."

"She's probably dead by now," said What-the-Dickens hotly. "Her name was Pepper." He realized his mistake. "*Is* Pepper. Her name is Pepper."

"She didn't quite have the goods, did she?" remarked Doctor Ill.

What-the-Dickens construed this as a question, and answered it. "I think she did," he stated. "She took care of me when we first met, though I'm sure I dragged her down. Then in her makeup mission, she was given a second assignment. We even managed to finish that task, too, and get back on time. I mean, I did, on her behalf."

So I've decided not to lie, he observed to himself. *Well, might as well be banished for telling the truth.*

"You worked together."

"Is that such a big deal? You gave her two missions: two agents working together did the job. Two equals two."

"Hmm," said Old Flossie. "They say a lot of things about what equals what, but does it add up to anything? Stuff and nonsense. Math is a myth, as Doctor Ill always says."

"Well, together we fulfilled her requirements," continued What-the-Dickens. "So though she is presumed dead by now, I want to petition that Pepper be granted her license anyway."

Doctor Ill's eyebrows went up. "What good does it do to grant a license to a corpse?"

"Honor," said What-the-Dickens. "Honor, and memory, I guess."

"Forget it," said the crown. "You're getting above yourself, little orphan boy. Leaving your wild calculations aside, you might as well know that I set her a daunting task to teach her a lesson. To fulfill two missions — intentionally sited at a great distance one from the other — was a virtual impossibility. She couldn't achieve those tasks even with your illegal help."

"But she did — or we did, I mean," he said.

"I don't believe you."

"Are you saying you set her up to fail?"

"She needed taking down a peg. She

didn't have the right stuff, I'm afraid, and I had to prove it to her. If you come back in her stead, with both teeth claimed at the correct outlets—well, it only proves you cheated in some way. It isn't possible for a skibberee to cover so much ground in such a short time."

"Well, I had help," he began to explain. "The slipstream of a truck on the highway—and a bird of my acquaintance—"

"You protest none of my assertions, I see. Also you proudly claim credit for breaking the rules. Skibbereen don't work in pairs and they don't accept help from strangers." Doctor Ill rubbed the back of one of his ears and looked weary.

"A truck isn't alive, and the bird was no stranger; she was my stepmother, in a very incidental manner—"

"We don't *accept help*. I appreciate that you're a slow learner, and inexperienced in the ways of our trade, but even so."

"All these rules. You train up Agents of Change," he begged. "So, why not change?"

"Silence." This was not so much thundered as sighed. "I can see I'm going to have to discuss colony policy with you if *you're* to be an Agent of Change."

"What?" said What-the-Dickens.

"Ask no questions," said Old Flossie automatically, though she sounded surprised herself.

"Well, it appears there is a position open," said Doctor Ill. "You'll be on probation, of course. It takes a while to get licensed. But you seem like Agent material."

As simple as that. I'm in, he thought.

"You've got something rather magnificent in your arms," continued the crown. "Tribute, I imagine. What is it?"

"The tooth of a wild beast."

Doctor Ill scratched the stump of one of his missing legs. "Where did you come across it?"

"I extracted it from the mouth of a tiger."

"Hah! A likely story. Still, it's impressive." Doctor Ill picked it up and whistled at the weight. He tilted the tiger tooth toward the cage where his mouse was penned.

The mouse reared back in terror, squeaking.

"This could come in handy, I see," said Doctor Ill ruminatively. "If we ever found ourselves needing to attack another colony, we could mount this on a stake and carry it like a totem. It would terrify those libertines over at Watermill Corners."

"If we're so small—so fragile—why do we attack one another's colonies?"

"It's the economy, stupid," said Old Flossie. "Supply and demand and consolidation of resources. It's all an accounting problem when you get down to it." She sounded somewhat tired, for the first time. "All in good time, you'll learn. Little by little. Small doesn't mean tender."

"It doesn't add up," said What-the-Dickens forthrightly.

"What does?" she snapped back. "That things should 'add up' is a whole lot of hooey, if you ask me."

"If we're so small and scared and mean," countered the orphan skibberee, "why do we bother? Why do we do it? Why do we put wishes in the way of humans, where they can find them and use them? To spend our time that way seems too noble, when those humans hardly deserve wishes of any kind!"

Doctor Ill had finished tucking the tiger tooth on a shelf of mementos, where it looked truly terrifying. But his expression, when he turned back, was anything but dreadful.

"Dear boy," he said. "It is really very simple. We plant the possibility of wishes coming true only in the paths of human children. Children still trust that when they wish on something bright—a birthday candle, a penny in a fountain—"

"A shooting star," interjected Old Flossie.

"—that their wish will come true. Wishing is the beginning of imagination. They practice wishing when they are young things, and then—when they have grown—they have a developed imagination. Which can do some harm—greed, that kind of thing—but more often does them some good. They can imagine that things might be different. Might be other than they seem. Could be better."

"But what is in it for us?" demanded What-the-Dickens. By now he was cross nearly to the point of tears. "Everything in our life is a trade, I've learned. What do we get out of it?"

Neither Old Flossie nor Doctor Ill spoke for a moment. "It cheapens skibbereen to talk about it," said the stump mistress in something of a growl. "We struggle to be proud, even if we'll never be mighty. The truth is this: We skibbereen have very little lives, but see—we can sometimes do some good."

"And why do we bother?" concluded

Doctor Ill, rhetorically. "I don't really know. Because it helps our little lives seem less small, perhaps. That is all.

"Anyway"—he clapped his hands, startling Muzzlemutt—"welcome to our small, small life here at Undertree Common. May you be as happy as it is socially useful to be."

He looked as if he were about to grasp What-the-Dickens's hands. But skibbereen don't touch each other, as Pepper had often said, so Doctor Ill merely clasped his own hands and rubbed them vigorously, as if congratulating himself on his speechifying.

"What I'm wondering about Pepper—" began What-the-Dickens. Before he could stutter his question to its conclusion, however, the fireflies in wall recesses began, suddenly and in unison, to blink. They flashed a sequence of cool-water colors, from baby blue to electrified cobalt.

"Blue alert!" brayed Old Fossie.

"Enemies!" hissed Doctor Ill, nearly turning blue himself. "Foreign agents breaching our borders! To your stations, kinmates!"

What-the-Dickens, still rubbing his wing tips in disbelief, was abandoned as Old Flossie and Doctor Ill half ran, half flew, so helter-skelter that it was more like skelter-helter. Right out the door of the office. This is to say, Old Flossie ran and Doctor Ill flew, for although he lacked the use of his legs, his wings still worked just fine.

Enemy attack! thought What-the-Dickens. *So soon after being conscripted. Wouldn't you know it.*

Could it be a ruse to test my civic loyalty? That would be just like them. . . .

Nonetheless, he hurried up to the cage of the mouse. He fiddled with the gate and flung it open. "You better skedaddle while the ske-daddling is possible."

But the mouse had been in captivity too long, and he was terrified of the tiger tooth. Of course he would be! Mice didn't even like cat's teeth, did they, and this was a tooth of the crown cat.

What-the-Dickens didn't have time to be persuasive. "Sorry, mate," he said to the wee timorous beastie. "The coast is clear, so I've gotta scram. Best of luck to you and all that."

The mouse said, *Luck? What's luck?* No one heard him but What-the-Dickens. But the orphan skibberee could not afford the time to decide whether he was imaging what animals could think or he was actually hearing them. The alarms were now blinking in the corridors as he hurried after the crown and the stump mistress. Flashes of acid yellow striped the blackout darkness.

❧ TWENTY-TWO ❧

What-the-Dickens caught up with Doctor Ill and Old Flossie as they skirted the edge of the auditorium.

Dozens, maybe hundreds of skibbereen had already rushed into the semi-darkness, linking their arms and swaying back and forth. Onstage, Silviana was carrying on as best she could given that the props of doll head and toothbrush brigade were absent. "The scientist, see, had a problem with his overbite as well as a pair of rogue incisors, see. His diction was lousy. . . . Edith didn't hear 'true fritillary.' She thought he said, 'Tooth fairy.'"

"Tooth fairy," murmured the audience, pacified just enough to keep from screaming.

Silviana gestured to Doctor Ill by shaking her hands theatrically; she seemed to be saying, *Release me from this obligation!* But perhaps she was just saying, *Stay and see how well I can perform under duress!*

As he followed along, What-the-Dickens couldn't help thinking that it was easier for him to guess at the perceptions of animals than at the thoughts of his own kind.

Silviana looked worried. But how could that be? She had no doubt.

What-the-Dickens pursued Doctor Ill and his associate as they plunged into a dark passage corkscrewing downward.

"Where are we going?" he asked, when he finally caught up with them on the straight-away.

"You? I didn't call for you," said Doctor Ill. "Well, you can help by lending some mus-cle, as long as you're here. We're going to sneak a good look from the observation deck and see if we can determine the nature of the invasion. I hope it's not that ghoulish colony over at the human cemetery."

"Grave End, you mean," interjected Old Flossie.

"Right. Northwest Sector, Division X. They're a morbid and a bellicose lot, and they've had designs on our digs for a while."

"Doctor Ill, surely our sentries in the field

would have given an earlier alarm?" asked Old Flossie.

"Unless they've been dealt with by superior forces mounting a surprise attack," said Doctor Ill coolly. "It's been known to happen."

They reached a tall shaft, greenly lit. What-the-Dickens guessed it must be a hollowed-out tree that hadn't yet fully died. The circumference of the shaft wasn't wide enough for a skibberee to open his or her wings to fly straight up. Instead, the shaft was supplied with a makeshift elevator.

Old Flossie climbed into a bucket made out of a paper coffee cup, with a picture of the Parthenon printed on it in deep blue ink. Several pieces of dental floss, threaded and knotted through holes punched beneath the ribbed rim of the cup, rose up into darkness overhead. Other pieces—perhaps the returning ends of those same ascending strands—hung down. These dangling strands finished in nets fastened around small stones, which hung like the several pendulums of stilled clocks.

"If you're coming, come; put your back into it," cried Old Flossie to What-the-Dickens. He climbed aboard.

"Wait," called a voice. Silviana appeared, flustered and out of breath.

"You're supposed to be distracting the timid," snapped Doctor Ill. "Are you abandoning your station?"

"I have no doubt," said Silviana, and she climbed aboard without waiting to be invited.

"Six, sixteen, seventy-six, heave!" cried Old Flossie. What-the-Dickens watched what the others did, and he did the same. He grabbed a pebble-cord and pulled it hand over hand, looping the cord about his forearm. They all let the pebbles drop below, and the cup lifted jerkily up. Hand over hand they hoisted themselves aloft, using pulleys mounted overhead.

"Don't go! I'm coming too!" screamed yet another voice, and Clea—the banker with the pipe-cleaner spectacles—appeared beneath them. But she was clocked by one of the lowering pebbles, and they heard no more from her after that.

"It's been years since a breach of our defenses," muttered Old Flossie between her teeth. "I never thought I'd live to see the day when it happened again. I wanted to be dead by now."

"Shut up," counseled Doctor Ill between gritted teeth.

They reached a landing station—an old knothole in the trunk. They looped the cords tightly around the thread spools nailed laterally in place for just such a docking maneuver.

Then, one by one, they climbed out through the knothole onto a limb that served as a lookout high above the stump.

"Oh, mercy's sakes," said Doctor Ill.

It took What-the-Dickens a few seconds to make out what was mesmerizing the others.

The body of a skibberee was laid to rest on the stump runway, curled up on itself.

"It's Pepper!" cried What-the-Dickens. Old Flossie whirled on him and slapped him across the face, then whipped a finger to her lips, indicating *Silence!*

What-the-Dickens tried to brush past the crown, but Doctor Ill put a strong hand on his shoulder. "It's not safe; it could be a trap," he whispered.

"You're not supposed to touch me. Let go. She might still be alive!" said What-the-Dickens, and broke free.

"It's the wind shaking her corpse. You're mistaken. Don't you dare," advised Doctor Ill, but the rogue skibberee did dare. He threw himself off the limb and swept in a descending half circle, coming neatly to rest on the runway. *My landing has improved,* he thought. *For once I didn't collapse on her and hurt her. Anyway, maybe she's already dead.*

"Pepper! Speak to me," said What-the-Dickens. But Pepper seemed to be beyond language.

Had she been able to fly home on a damaged wing? It must have taken everything out of her. Had she then perished on her own doorstep, of fatigue and war wounds?

Skibbereen don't touch each other. He knew that now, but he felt her wings anyway. They were cool and dry, like silk leaves.

But her slim wrist was still warm. What did it mean?

"She needs your attention, Doctor Ill," called What-the-Dickens. "She might still be alive. I can't tell."

He looked up. Even knowing what the crown looked like, and where he stood, What-the-Dickens couldn't locate Doctor Ill among the foliage. How well a motionless skibberee is camouflaged. . . . Hidden, and forbidden.

There was no sound of the footfall of infantrymen, no buzz of skibbereen attacking from the air. Only the morning wind among leaves, the hoot of a car horn on the cloverleaf, the belch of a frog digesting a bit too much swamp water.

Doctor Ill will be torn, thought What-the-Dickens. *He's not a bad skibberee, and he has a weight on his shoulders. The good of the colony is his obligation.*

And perhaps he thinks it is a trap. After all, something *set off some alarm or other.*

But here she is, trembling in the dawn light, alive or dead or halfway in between. Even if she has been stripped of her name, and her chances of advancement.

"She's one of ours," he called again. "Please." Then, courteously and in case it made a difference, he corrected himself. "She's one of yours. Even if she's dead, she belongs to the Undertree Common in a way I never will, even now."

"Aha," said a voice like thunder. "It's true! There are more of you!"

What-the-Dickens felt a striated cloud made of clammy pinkish ham close about him. He nearly passed out from the smell of pencil shavings, Ivory soap, buttered toast, and last year's acorns penned up in a cigar box. The smell, you guessed it, of human boy.

It must be Gage. Gage Tavenner. That kid Gage had brought Pepper back. Did he mean to exchange a dead skibberee for a live one? He was cupping What-the-Dickens in his moist hands, lifting him in the air, and bringing him near the furnace of peanut butter breath.

"She *said* there were more," said Gage. "Hi, you."

"Let him go," came a small but bellowing voice. The crown was breaking silence. Breaking the rules. "Put him down, you overgrown cad."

"Another one! The place is crawling with them," said Gage.

Doctor Ill darted into view and took up a military position. His porcupine cane doubled conveniently as a rapier.

What-the-Dickens rubbed his eyes. The crown was flanked on one side by Silviana, prancing prettily in the air as if on an invisible miniature pony, and on the other side by Old Flossie, who proved it was possible for skibbereen of certain healthy proportions to hover with their arms folded across their bosoms.

Brave souls, he thought. *This Gage could wipe them out of the air with a single swipe of his elbow.*

"Leave him be. Just set him down gently and nothing will happen to you," said Doctor Ill. "Did you hear me, you lump? You lummox?"

"Okay, okay. Hold your horses." Gage set What-the-Dickens back down on the stump. The uppers from Undertree Common descended, and at touchdown took their places near the orphan skibberee. They stood together—rather uncomfortably close for skibbereen—as Gage in striped pajamas knelt in the weeds that grew near the stump.

"Will she be all right?" Gage asked. "Pepper, I mean? Did I get here in time?"

"She's brought danger to us all," said Doctor Ill. "She doesn't deserve to be all right. She betrayed us. Go away."

Gage put his smooth boy's chin right down on the stump. He was close enough that the skibbereen could have poked his eyes out if they'd been armed with sticks. "Fix her up!" he shouted, so loudly that Silviana sat down suddenly and made an unladylike noise in her skirts. Even Pepper's curled body rolled over in the force of Gage's shout.

"There are some things even wishes can't fix," asserted Doctor Ill. But he went forward to have a look at her body. What-the-Dickens couldn't see what the crown actually did—whether he had little vials of toothpaste in his vest pocket, or a healing touch with a gentle fist. But before long Pepper's wings, which had been curling up like dead leaves, began to relax and resume something of their original shape.

"Will she fly again?" asked Gage.

"She won't need to," answered Doctor Ill. "I've made her spine relax, and that's made her look calm. I can't make her live. We all have our duty, and she has a duty to die."

"But if she's alive, maybe she'll get better," said the boy. "Thanks to your help. Is she alive?"

Doctor Ill slapped his hands together as if disgusted with having actually touched a failing skibberee. "I've done what you asked," he said curtly. "I've earned your respect. Now you do the honorable thing and leave us alone."

Gage sat back on his heels. "Don't mind me; I'll just listen," he said. "That's all I want to do."

What-the-Dickens turned to the crown. "Why did you defend me? Why have you risked your life for me? What about 'hidden and forbidden'?"

"Asking *questions* again, are we?" queried Old Flossie, glowering.

Doctor Ill shushed the stump mistress, and said to What-the-Dickens, "Listen, little mushroom-head. You are worth too much to us to lose. If you could imagine how to harness a truck's tailwind to travel more swiftly—and if you could catch a ride from a grisset—well, you may be dumb as they come, but you've got *some* sort of cleverness about you. We can use your skills. It wasn't kindness on my part. It was conservation of our natural resources: yours."

"But you wouldn't come forward to save Pepper on *her* own merits," said What-the-Dickens.

"We can afford to live without Pepper if it's her time to die," said Silviana. "*That's* what they mean. You, you trickster, you're more valuable than you look." She added, apologetically, "You look like a shell-shocked dandelion."

"You'd let her die just because she's—ordinary?" asked Gage, a cloud of youthful outrage all but spitting upon them. What-the-Dickens had almost forgotten he was there: it was as if one of the heads on Mount Rushmore opened its mouth and admitted being irritated by a hiker near his chin.

"You, pipe down," cried Doctor Ill to Gage. "I'm tired of being pestered by a juvenile barbarian. And *you,* What-the-Difference! Your ignorance has stopped being comic and is become vexing. You know *nothing* of our society's traditions. Have you ever heard Silviana tell the story of the honorable death? No, of course not. You're from 'away.' Listen to me, you. A skibberee folds her wings when it's her time to die, and she doesn't ask for an exemption or a furlough. It isn't done. Her 'once upon a time' ends here."

"But you're a doctor," said What-the-Dickens. "You must see exceptions? Surely?"

"*Yours* is not to question the crown!" sang out Old Flossie, to a venomous melody.

"I'm a doctor, yes: a doctor of social policy and military strategy," continued Doctor Ill wearily. "And I rule out exceptions. She missed earning her license as an Agent of Change. Don't require that she also surrender her chance for an honorable death. That would add insult to injury, and be selfish of you."

"An honorable death?"

"We must do what we're told! In any community with as little chance of survival as ours, how would we maintain discipline if we made exceptions for every life? We are frail creatures—you're young and you don't know this yet. Don't make it worse for her. She fumbled; she failed. She had an accident. We accept, we move on—"

"It's also an accident that I was born an orphan," replied What-the-Dickens, "and that I missed out on all the early training. I can't help it if I can imagine that maybe she doesn't really need to die. I didn't learn all that the very moment I was born. I haven't mastered that lesson yet."

What-the-Dickens came forward again. Now he knelt beside Pepper. Now he stroked her brow. It was as if she was sleeping, very deeply but peacefully. She looked as peppery as usual, only less present somehow.

The crown's voice became more sympathetic. "You are too young to know the story about death. I see that now."

"Is there a different story for her, then? Pepper, can you hear me? Listen: A new chapter in the Duty Pageant. A new duty put upon us: to make it. Are you listening? Not once upon a time, but, oh, *next* upon a time. Next upon a time, Pepper stirred from her torpor. She woke up, blinking in the light, and—and—"

Storytelling wasn't one of his hidden talents.

"— and it felt okay. And she got up and, um, moved around some."

"Stop that," said Doctor Ill. "Mawkish fool. No one gave you the right to make up nonsense. You'll regret it."

"Let him talk," said Gage, putting his hand out to form a wall that gave What-the-Dickens and Pepper some privacy behind it. It was like *One Hundred Years of Solitude* without the solitude.

"Pepper," said What-the-Dickens, and he licked her wing tips, both of them. They had the flavor of salt tears cut with lemon.

"I've had enough out of you," cried Doctor Ill. Bravely and rashly, he rushed toward Gage's hand.

"Ow. Did you *sting* me? I didn't know you could do that," said Gage, removing his hand in a rush.

"Me either," said What-the-Dickens, impressed.

"You're not the only one with hidden talents," growled the crown. "Hidden and forbidden. But useful at times. Comes from a life in the service."

Old Flossie sighed. "You're lucky that human is just a kitten or he'd have squashed us all flat just then." Gage was busy hopping up and down with his stung hand tucked in his armpit.

"All is lost," said Doctor Ill. "Come now, while the human menace is distracted. We must abandon hope, we must abandon the remains of the invalid. We must fly and reestablish ourselves elsewhere. What-the-Dickens, come."

"Come with us," said Silviana. She reached out her perfect hand to him. "I need you. We need you." The orphan looked up at her. "Do good where it can still be done," said Silviana. "Here. With us."

Doctor Ill had flown to the fungus that disguised the portal entrance. Rashly he flung it aside. "We are lost. We are ruined. Let's scram," he said.

But Gage put his hand on the fungus and clamped it back into place. "You don't have to fly," said the human boy. "I won't squeal. Your secret's safe with me. Really. Pepper told me everything, all about your colony, and the tooth plantation, and the wishing candles. I can see why it's so important. I won't tell."

"You know too much," said Old Flossie. "You have to die." She looked at Doctor Ill. "You have anything stronger in the poison department?"

"Oh, I'll die eventually," said Gage without distress. "But I can keep a secret until then."

"Humans can't keep secrets," said Doctor Ill, spitting. "Don't get me started. Humans do nothing but chatter from the cradle to the grave."

"So how are you going to kill me? Sting me to death? I hope not. Slash my ankles with a porcupine needle? Tattoo me to death with poison ivy juice?"

"Could we buy his silence?" asked Pepper in a quavery tone as she tried to sit up.

What-the-Dickens said her name. Once, twice, then again.

He fell on his knees to give her a hug, but she said, "Gentle! I'm not myself," and he held back. Maybe she meant she wasn't Pepper anymore. Then who could she be?

"You're alive," he said, "and you're home."

"I'm lingering," she corrected him, "and I'm still here. For now."

"We haven't much time," said Silviana. "Skibbereen are never seen, and the sun is getting higher." She mimed the sun mounting in the sky, though they could all see it for themselves: a white burning hole punched in the pale blue.

"I mean it," Pepper said. Her voice came out as a papery rustle. "Listen to me. Gage was good enough to carry me here, since I can't fly — or I couldn't, anyway." She flexed her bad wing. It still had a rip in it, but the frame and struts seemed more or less intact. "I owe him big-time, so I gotta trade him something. Maybe I could trade him extra, and buy his silence."

"I doubt that would work," said Old Flossie. "Humans are tricksy creatures and never keep their end of a promise."

"Try me," said Gage, but no one paid him any attention.

"Besides," said Pepper, "now I know what the human wants."

"What?" asked Doctor Ill, Old Flossie, and What-the-Dickens all at the same time. Even Gage was listening curiously.

"He paid close attention to what I told him about the Undertree Common. He wanted to hear about all my earlier missions and assignments. He wanted to know everything about other folks. He is in love with stories and words and all that kind of thing." Pepper rolled her eyes.

"Could we give him Silviana?" mused Old Flossie. "I've gone off her a bit, anyway." Silviana sulked, not quite so prettily as usual, and made a face.

"No," said What-the-Dickens. "No hostages! Are you crazy?"

"Besides," said Doctor Ill, "Silviana has a name, and she's earned it. She's a star."

"Do I get a say?" asked Gage. "You're right about the stories, incidentally. I don't have enough to read. But I don't want to take another captive. Are you kidding? McCavity is more trouble than she's worth already. I wish I could liberate *her*. That's why I brought Pepper back in the first place. I don't want to imprison anyone else. That nasty cat is more pet than I can handle as it is."

What-the-Dickens felt the smallest twinge, a kind of memory of hope, for some old belief that used to be called McCavity. But that longing sizzled out. McCavity had been his first big mistake. There was no need to repeat it.

"I have an idea," said What-the-Dickens. "Or I almost do." He puzzled over the math of it in his head. This plus this equals that plus that. Or does it? "Do you know a child named Lee Gangster? Cowboy pajamas, missing front tooth?"

"I never met the pajamas. But sure, I know him. In my classroom, his desk is right next to mine."

"Well," said What-the-Dickens, "he has an ancient grandmother with a mess of poetry books she can't stand. Maybe she would trade you her books."

"Trade? But for what?"

"For McCavity. Didn't you say you wanted to get rid of her?"

Gage looked stunned. "Do you think old Mrs. Gangster would really do that?"

"You could ask her. She'll be much nicer to you if she doesn't think you're the Fairy of Death come to take her soul away."

"I *can* act kind of human," said Gage. "With a little practice, I mean."

"So that's all settled," said Pepper.

"No, it isn't," said Doctor Ill, who was pinching the finger of one hand with the fingers of his other hand and looking befuddled. "Our rogue skibberee, What's-the-Use, has negotiated a trade. It's all very sweet, all hearts and ribbons and such, but it has nothing to do with us, and doesn't solve our problem."

He didn't so much glare at Pepper as wince in her direction. "You still sang like a canary in a cage. You told too much. You are banished, and as for this human—well, I was being crude when I said he had to die. But we're ruined here. We'll have to mount a campaign and invade those creeps over at Grave End. Big military maneuvers. Attack, fall back, attack. Ugh, and live among all those granite headstones with the dreadful carved angels. Too depressing. And the loss of life in an invasion. Think of it. Not to mention the trouble of packing."

"Do you think I'd ever tell anyone that I talked to tooth fairies?" said Gage. "Really, I'd be labeled such a loser. Or worse. Can't you just trust me?"

"I wish I could. But humans are notoriously untrustworthy, and we're not about to start now. Old Flossie, go call up the home guard. We evacuate at sunset."

"Wait," said What-the-Dickens. "Wait. I have an idea."

They waited.

"Bring us a candle," he said at last. "Bring us a full-moon-grown birthday candle. Gage can light it, and he can make a wish, and then he will blow the candle out."

"So what?" said Doctor Ill. "What will that solve?"

"Depending on what the wish is," said What-the-Dickens, thinking slowly and carefully—for he knew he had a plodding mind—"perhaps everything. If what we need is that he had never found out about us—"

The morning wind swayed the branches, rustling.

Light billowed. Was that a scatter of June petals, with June scent? Little confetti dots of ripped white blossom on the breeze.

Away, a grisset trashed some summer melody, but good.

"I think I see what you're getting at," said Gage. For a mountain of a kid his voice could go soft and throaty. "I could wish"—and he gulped once or twice—"that I'd forget I ever met any of you."

"Uncommonly decent," said Doctor Ill. "Hardly human, in fact."

Old Flossie poked Doctor Ill in the ribs. "Don't trust him. Why would he do that? What good could that possibly do him?"

"It would do *you* good," said Gage. "I don't need to be paid for that. I mean, really."

Have I got this right? wondered What-the-Dickens. *The possibility of wishing strengthens the imagination to consider, at times, that things could improve. Could be different. They could. They might.*

"You better hurry before I change my mind," warned Gage. "I'm trying to be decent here, but I'm not a saint."

Doctor Ill signaled behind his back, and Old Flossie scurried away. "What if we bring you a candle and you wish for something else?" said the crown. "What if you wish all skibbereen were ninety feet tall and yodeled as they flew?"

"I'm not cruel, and I'm not stupid," said Gage.

"He isn't either of those," said Pepper.

"But you must wish to remember my idea about trading McCavity for the books," said What-the-Dickens. "If anyone could master that bewitching cat of yours, it's old Mrs. Lee

Gangster. She might be an ancient monster in her own right, but she's lonely. And she could terrorize McCavity as much as McCavity deserves it."

Gage sat down next to the stump. He brought his face close to the tree trunk and looked at Doctor Ill, Pepper, and What-the-Dickens. "I'm trying to remember you as hard as I can before I make a wish to forget you just as hard," he said. His eyes, I must admit, were not entirely dry. "Can you just answer me something? Even if I only get to know it for a little while?"

Doctor Ill, as graciously as he could, said, "Oh, go on, then. Ask."

"Why are you so eager to give us human beings wishes?" asked young Gage. "It's one thing that Pepper couldn't explain."

"That's classified," said Doctor Ill. "Released only on a need-to-know basis, and you don't need to know. I may be grateful to you, but I'm not giving away state secrets here, you big clod."

"Well, tell me this, then," said Gage. "Teenagers always make fun of kids believing in tooth fairies. How can you stand it?"

"Skibbereen," said Silviana, "if you want to

use the correct term. Skibbereen are never seen." She flounced, to be seen.

"We don't protest what we can't change," said Doctor Ill. "Besides, a little misinformation can help clear away any residual memory of teeth and wishes, or the rare occasional glimpse by a human child of a skibberee Agent of Change. Children talk themselves out of their convictions as they grow up and become distracted by their huge selfish selves. All the literature is consistent on this point. Children begin to think they've imagined us."

"I won't," said Gage. "Forgive me," he remarked, blowing his nose on his pajama sleeve. "I've spent an awful lot of my life being lonely and bored, and it's sad to meet you all, and learn there is a full city of skibbereen within walking distance, only to say good-bye so soon."

"But I'll never forget *you*," said Pepper.

"And I'll never forget you either," said What-the-Dickens.

"Ah, here she is. The stump mistress can really move when she's on a mission," said Doctor Ill. Old Flossie, breathing heavily, had a newly harvested candle under one arm. Under the other, she carried a book of matches that spelled out, in curly red script,

LUCIANO'S RISTORANTE

FAMILIES WELCOME

"I hope this works," she said, when she could catch her breath.

"I hope so too," said What-the-Dickens, but he was partly lying.

"Can I say good-bye?" said Gage Tavenner.

"Better not to," said Doctor Ill. "Just do your job, fellow. It'll all be over soon. I should say, if you carry this out, you'll be teaching me something new about human honor. If you fail, of course, I'll hate you, and I'll hunt you down, and find a way to kill you."

They all looked at him. "You know, for a little fellow, you're a big bully," said Gage.

"I take that as a compliment," said Doctor Ill briskly. "Come now, let's not dawdle. The sun dries out our wings, and this chapter is almost over."

Pepper managed to get to her feet. She and What-the-Dickens held the candle up between them.

Old Flossie opened up the book of matches so Doctor Ill could extract one. Then she followed the directions on the matchbook cover that said, *Close cover before striking.* "Wouldn't want the whole rotten stump to become an inferno now," she explained. "Not when we've gotten this far."

"I've only done this once or twice," said Doctor Ill. "I beg your patience."

"I can light a match," said Gage. "Let me."

"Human children don't light matches in the woods; it isn't done," said the crown. "You better practice your wish in your head. Are you ready?"

Gage closed his eyes and nodded, but then he opened them again. He didn't want to waste one short second of seeing the skibbereen assembled there on the sawed stump.

Doctor Ill held the match straight out in the air, like a sword, and he began to spin. He rotated faster than What-the-Dickens had imagined possible. The crown shaped his wings cleverly to catch the wind, like a pinwheel.

Soon he was moving so fast that his body was just a blur. The revolving match looked like a kind of red-tipped skirt flaring out from Doctor Ill's rotund waist. When the match head made contact with the sulfur strip at last, Doctor Ill braked wildly. Careering this way and that, he corrected his balance, with the lit match raised like a torch over his head.

"He's a born leader," murmured Old Flossie admiringly.

"I have no doubt," said Silviana, in tremors of feeling.

Doctor Ill flew forward and lit the candle, and What-the-Dickens and Pepper lifted it up between them, the nearer to Gage's breath.

"I wish," said Gage, and his voice caught in his throat.

They waited. "Do go on, before we're scalded with melting wax," said Pepper.

"I wish . . ." he tried again, and he couldn't continue. But then the first drop of melted wax did fall from the candle, and stuck Pepper on her wounded wing. She screamed in pain and staggered.

"Oh, bother," said Gage. "I wish that I forget I ever met any of you but that I remember your idea about trading McCavity for the old lady's books!"

He blew the candle out. He blew so hard that all five of the skibbereen tumbled off the stump, along with the dead leaves and the pine cone. They fell to the far side.

There they waited in silence, in the cooling shadow of the dead tree.

Five green thoughts in a green shade.

Gage sat down on the stump and, because he thought he was alone and no one could see him, he cried a little bit, from loneliness. This was not the first time he had ever done this, and it wouldn't be the last.

Then he got up and shuffled through the old weeds, and when he was sure no traffic was coming, he darted across the highway ramp. He went home. That is, they guessed he went home. They didn't know for sure. They never saw him again.

"Now what?" said What-the-Dickens. "What next for us?"

"Which us? What *us*?" asked Old Flossie and Doctor Ill, simultaneously. Silviana added, "Hello?" and moved forward, putting her hand attractively to her brow as if seeing future history.

"Us two," said What-the-Dickens. He pointed first at Pepper and then at himself.

"I got no prospects," complained Pepper. "Don't spend your hopes on me, What-the-Dickens. I don't know how poorly off I am. I might not last. I don't feel so hot. I don't know how long I'm gonna live."

"Neither do I," said What-the-Dickens. "I never have known that. So we're at the same starting place, right now. We can find out together, by ourselves. Let's go."

Pepper groaned and began to raise herself to her feet. What-the-Dickens rushed to help, but she stayed his hand. "Excuse me, if I'm going to stand on my own feet, I'm going to stand on my own feet."

"May I ask a question?" Doctor Ill sounded faint. "Together? But we need you at Undertree Common, What-the-Dickens."

"Us two," said What-the-Dickens. "We're not colony material. We're moving out. We'll take our chances abroad."

He pointed to Pepper. She grinned back at him and made her mouth look as if she had swallowed a boomerang—a sort of sideways smile, a smirk of huge disbelief. "Us two," he repeated. "I never should have abandoned Pepper, valuing her honor more than her life. Biggest mistake I ever made. But I'm not going to do it again. We'll find our own way out into the world."

"You can't live outside of a colony. It can't be done. Life is full of danger. The world is treacherous. Pitfalls abound. Temptations on all sides. Your only hope is to keep apart—hidden and forbidden."

"I've kept apart already," said What-the-Dickens. "And I've lived outside of a colony already, too. I've already done it. We can manage. We'll be all right. We're just going to govern ourselves."

"You're a traitor," said Doctor Ill, in shock and admiration.

"Together," insisted the orphan. "One and one. One plus one. Makes two. Us two."

"He's a genius," cried Old Flossie. Silviana caught the stump mistress as she fainted dead away at the higher math of it all.

❖ ❖ ❖

Then they turned, all heads at once, at a noise from down the slope. An animal with a low, long cough? . . . A skirring as of tires on mud? . . . It was hard to say. But that they could hear it at all, from their beleaguered aerie, brought home the truth: the winds had dropped. Other sounds could sound.

They rose from their slumped positions on the floor and looked out the window. The sky was grim putty, but a localized glow burnished the mist from below. Turned it whiter. The steamy fog in the valley was lifting.

"Mommy," said Rebecca Ruth. The anxiety and need in her voice was too baldly stated to ignore; they all caught the shiver. And maybe that diffuse light *could* be a battered car's single working headlight, one that had gotten raked askew by difficult driving conditions.

Or it could be the deputies returning. Or looters working their way up the slope—though looters were less scary now that dawn was near. "Don't hold your breath," said Gage. "If it's a traveler coming here by car, they'll have to go the long way around when they find the bluff road collapsed halfway down the hill."

Rebecca Ruth, good for so long, began at last to weep with abandon. She threw her head against the back of the couch, resisting the cuddles of her family. "Mommy," she cried, over and over. " 'Becca want Mommy."

Who doesn't? thought Dinah. But hug her baby sister as hard as she could, she couldn't console her. Rebecca Ruth had been patient long enough. She thrashed and sorrowed and bit at the world.

"Let's get that little lady some food," said Gage. "Who needs ratty old tooth fairies when your stomach is rumbling. That's what I say." He stood up. "We have two candy bars."

The kitchen radio, suddenly and without warning, kicked on. A table lamp's glare seared the room.

Just for an instant before the power cut out again, they all caught a voice, ravishingly clear, funneling from the world beyond them. ". . . when the National Weather Service will next be reporting on this region, but from the WCXN studios near the top of Mount Raparus, folks, as I live and breathe, the naked eye sees light. A little south of us, word is that storm-related damage took out . . ."

Then it was gone, that beautiful noise. The table lamp went grey, leaving a greenish after-image in their greedy eyes. But the interruption had startled Rebecca Ruth into silence, and before she could return to her crying, Dinah exclaimed, "It's Rebecca Ruth's birthday today! Let's do the cake now, before—before—"

"Before we're taken away," said Zeke. "Good idea."

"Birfday cake," agreed Rebecca Ruth, sniffling, agreeing to be mollified.

And it was something to do, just for a moment, while the light that they'd seen took time to strengthen and turn into something one way or the other.

Gage said, "Look, it is light enough now. That means that your birthday has come, Rebecca Ruth. Thanks to your disobedient rapscallion loving kind of brother, you have a funny. Little. Birthday. CAKE. Can you believe it? Also that scrap of an orphaned candle Dinah found in the pantry. So we'll have birthday cake for breakfast. We'll get it going now. Shall we?"

"I'll get the candle," said Dinah.

"I'll light it," said Zeke.

"We'll all sing the song," said Gage.

"Me me me," said Rebecca Ruth, meaning, I'll blow the candle out. And hurry.

"Hold your horses," said Gage. "You'll be two for, let me do the math, the next third of your life so far. So learn patience."

He then said, "Patience. The thing I've just run out of. Zeke, will you take a turn to change your sister? We'll get the cake ready."

Zeke saw to Rebecca Ruth's makeshift diapers. While Dinah escaped to the kitchen with Gage to get the supplies ready, she could hear her brother talking to the birthday girl, and she watched them out of the corner of her eye.

"Look," Zeke was saying, bouncing and jouncing his baby sister. "You're two years old today, on a day that starts without rain! Is that a good sign or what?"

Rebecca Ruth didn't reply. She only ever spoke when she felt like it.

Zeke said, "You're one of the baby saints, Rebecca Ruth. Everything gets better now that you're two and ready to take over the world."

Well, somebody ought to, thought Dinah. Rebecca Ruth might be no worse at ruling the world than everyone else was proving to be.

With the flat edge of the knife, Gage repaired the iffy frosting. "It's not much to look at, but it does qualify as cake," he finally said. "It'll have to do."

"Do you think there is more to the story?" asked Dinah.

"Which story?" asked Gage.

"You're teasing me," she said. "You're pretending to forget. That's mean and rude."

"Yes, I'm teasing you," he admitted. "Well, cut me some slack; I've been talking all night long, and I'm bushed. Of course there is more to the story: They're alive. They lasted. But I don't know what their story says next. I doubt that What-the-Dickens and Pepper ever went back to Undertree Common, however."

"Where else could they go? Her wing was busted."

"But that melted wax from the candle dripped on it. Maybe it sealed over the wound, and she found she could fly again. Anyway, I've always wondered if they went back to old Lee Gangster's room for her pair of dentures. Of course they'd have to brave McCavity to get in there, but just think what they could do with a whole set of false teeth."

"McCavity would cream them if she saw them again." Dinah narrowed her eyes—like a cat's. "Hey, did you give McCavity to old Mrs. Gangster? And get her boring old poetry books in return?"

"I did indeed," said Gage. "But I can't tell you how the idea popped into my head to arrange it." He leaned over the sink and wiped the kitchen window clear with the palm of his hand. "They could scare McCavity with the tiger tooth, if they got their hands on it. It belonged to What-the-Dickens. It was his crown jewel, in a way."

"Cool," said Dinah. "But the two little skibbereen couldn't manage to fly with something as heavy as old-lady dentures, even between them."

"True." Gage licked the knife the way a kid would. "But remember that What-the-Dickens had seen Pepper use dental floss as a lasso and a rappelling rope. She was mighty talented too, in her way. And kind of brave."

"Kind of? Very brave. She dived in to save What-the-Dickens from McCavity. But I can't see them managing to hoist dentures all by themselves."

"Well, he knew how to put two and two together. . . . Hey, and besides, he did seem to have a capacity, perhaps a mutant skill, in talking to animals. He could locate the rust-throated grisset. She could help lift the false teeth off Lee Gangster's windowsill."

"I know why he could hear Maharajah when no one else could," said Dinah.

"You do?" Gage was amazed. "I never could figure that out. Was it a miracle?"

"Depends on your definition of miracle," she said, feeling smart. "Use your good mind. Remember, skibbereen learn their language fast, from the first words their mothers say. What's the first word What-the-Dickens heard?"

"I forget."

"Meow. From McCavity. So the orphan skibberee was primed right from the start to be able to hear what no one else could. He had the right ear to hear it."

"That's called faith," rang out Zeke, from the other room, but not sounding so argumentative as he had earlier. "Hah—so in the end, it was McCavity who gave the skibberee a present, not the other way around!"

"Touché," Gage called back, but he winked at Dinah. So Zeke had been listening.

Dinah continued. "And maybe What-the-Dickens and Pepper could get the teeth inside the stump, somehow, and scare that bossy old crown into releasing the mouse. Muzzlemutt."

"Doctor Ill wasn't so bad. Just doing his job. But I see what you mean. I've never been happy about that captive mouse, you know."

"Me either." Dinah took a turn to lick the knife. "Yuck. This frosting has seen better days."

"So have we all," said Gage.

"They didn't have much luck, those two," said

Dinah, as she centered the cake on a breadboard. "The whole world against them, really."

Gage was silent.

"What-the-Dickens and Pepper, I mean," she said. "I wasn't talking about, you know. Mommy and Dad. They have their own luck. And grace."

"I know," he said.

"But what did the skibbereen have going for them? Separated from the colony like that, and banished even from your boyhood memory."

"They were up against it. That's for sure. What a dreadful lot of accident: the orphan being born alone, and Pepper meeting up with McCavity. Everywhere you turn, trouble waiting with claws."

"A lot of accident out there to deal with." Dinah couldn't help waving her hand, indicating the ridge, the slope, the storm, the spoiled insulin, the mudslides, the whole enchilada.

"Accidents, and acts of the imagination," said Gage. "I guess that's how we make ourselves, and how we're made."

"Is it true?" She faced him and put out her hands, stalling his procession to the front room, where Rebecca Ruth was beginning to squirm and lose patience. "Is any of it true?"

"It was a story for a long night," he said. "I've been thinking of telling a story like that sometime, but I never had the chance to put it together before. What do you think?"

She tried to think:

+ Gage made up the story.
+ He didn't make up the story.
+ It could be true either way.

"I think it was true," she said. "I want it to be true. It was about you, after all."

"Yes," he replied, "but hey, I value the truth. Listen: If it were true, and I had made such a wish, I couldn't remember about Pepper and What-the-Dickens. Not even enough to make up a story about them. Because I wished to forget I ever met them."

"Maybe," said Dinah. She narrowed her eyes. "Or maybe you think you made it up, a whole act of the imagination, a 'once upon a time.' But maybe it really happened and you really have forgotten it, like you wished for. So what you think is a story you're making up is really something that really happened."

"Go to law school," he said. "I suppose if you're right, we'll never know."

"I could find out," she said. "I could look for them. I never made the promise that you made."

"If anyone could find out about them, it's you," Gage agreed. "You've got a big talent of attention; you proved that tonight. And you have the benefit of belief. Look close, and see what you find."

"The whole reason that tooth fairies give wish-es," she reminded him, using her good mind, "is to help us practice imagining a better world."

He looked at her, blinking rapidly, a bitter smile. Nodded: *Right*.

"But what did they do next? Did they go to a city? Did they locate another colony to take them in? Did they ever meet up with Doctor Ill and Silviana and the stump mistress again?"

"I don't know," admitted Gage. "I haven't told that story. Maybe you will have the chance to do that yourself."

Dinah thought about that. What a great reason to use her skill at numbering things. She tried to imagine the possibilities:

- ✦ Doctor Ill at an international conference of crowns.
- ✦ Silviana getting a virus and Old Flossie performing at the Duty Pageant.
- ✦ A midnight attack by those monsters over at Sequoia Heights.
- ✦ Or McCavity's revenge!
- ✦ Or how about the theft of George Washington's tooth?

She could almost see these moments in future skibbereen history. Not as visions, not as truth: as possibilities.

But when she thought about What-the-Dickens

and Pepper, and what they might do next, she couldn't actually see them. She saw only a level field in the dark, a field blurred with a haze of low light hovering about the height of dandelion heads. A meadow of wishes, a field of candles, all alight, burning through the wishing hour.

"Come on, sleepyhead," said Gage gently. "You're finally getting dozy. Let's get this song and dance over with."

They swung through the door. The baby's face was lit by the light of a single candle. She squirmed in Zeke's arms. Their voices sounded ragged, not much more melodic than that of a rust-throated grisset. Four tired voices in a storm, while the youngest among them clapped and was cheered.

Dinah leaned down as Rebecca Ruth got ready to blow out the candle. The new two-year-old might need some help. Dinah had a wish of her own ready, just in case.

I wish, she thought. *I wish: I wish . . .*

But she wouldn't even put it into words for herself: she would just wish it without words.

And may Brittney and Juliette be safe, she added in a sudden rush of P.S., an impromptu addendum, just in case it could still count.

Gage thought, *I believe in story. Zeke believes in prayer. Dinah believes in magic. Rebecca Ruth—who knows what Rebecca Ruth believes in?*

Rebecca Ruth believes in Rebecca Ruth. Who is to say that any single one of us is wrong?

Together, they faced the little candle. Confirmed in their own convictions, everyone in the room wished.

The big wind was over, but their four wishes made a little wind, coming from four directions at once. Which of their breaths extinguished the candle?

They couldn't tell. They would have to wait and see what came true.

– ACKNOWLEDGMENTS –

I owe thanks to a lot of people, he thought, hoping he could remember them all. He listed them:

+ Stephanie Loer of the Boston Globe for asking me to supply a serialized story ("Gangster Teeth") from which What-the-Dickens descends;
+ Elizabeth Bicknell for the exercise of her editorial craft, which in her hands becomes an art;
+ Natacha Liuzzi for a little quote-hunting in libraries and bookstores;
+ Betty Levin, my longtime first reader and commentator;
+ William Reiss of John Hawkins and Associates;
+ the good people of West Concord Union Church, in whose basement kitchen I was allowed to work;
+ Andy Newman, for brushing the kids' teeth while I took notes;
+ the following for their collective brilliance, referred to directly, allusively, or parodically, but always respectfully: the anonymous authors of the world of nursery rhymes; William Allingham; James Barrie; Robert Burns; Lewis Carroll; James Carville and George Stephanopoulos; the scriptwriters of Casablanca; Samuel Coleridge; Emily Dickinson; Robert Graves; Paul Heins; whoever adapted the line from Herodotus into the inscription on the Main Post Office, New York City; Madeleine L'Engle; Norman Maclean; J. G. Magee Jr., RCAF; Andrew Marvell; Edgar Lee Masters; Margaret Mitchell; Alfred Noyes; Carl Sandburg; William Shakespeare, who first used the phrase "what the dickens" in print; the Star Trek scriptwriters; Wallace Stevens; Dylan Thomas; and the script-writers of the 1950s Superman television series.